P. 56 č Joseph?

When did Idumean Convert?

Jesus Unbound

Richard D Malmed

authorHOUSE®

AuthorHouse™
1663 Liberty Drive
Bloomington, IN 47403
www.authorhouse.com
Phone: 1 (800) 839-8640

Published by AuthorHouse   10/14/2015

ISBN: 978-1-5049-5288-0 (sc)
ISBN: 978-1-5049-5289-7 (hc)
ISBN: 978-1-5049-5287-3 (e)

Library of Congress Control Number: 2015915983

Print information available on the last page.

This book is printed on acid-free paper.

Contents

Book One

Chapter One: Early Pilgrimage to Jerusalem.................................... 3
Chapter Two: Jesus Leaves Nazareth to Study 11
Chapter Three: Judas and Jesus in Judas' Home; Early Travels... 14
Chapter Four: Jesus and Judas Meet Essenes............................... 22
Chapter Five: Judas as Sicarii 28
Chapter Six: John the Baptist.. 34
Chapter Seven: Jesus Leaves John with Peter and Andrew.......... 40
Chapter Eight: Jesus Goes to Nazareth 43
Chapter Nine: Joseph at Caesarea.. 53
Chapter Ten: Pilate—Introduction 63
Chapter Eleven: Jesus—early visit to Bethany 68
Chapter Twelve: Lazarus and Jesus Talk of Mandrake 74
Chapter Thirteen: Kaiaphas meets Pilate 76
Chapter Fourteen: News of Lazarus' "Death" 82

Book Two

Chapter One: Jesus' Entry into Jerusalem 89
Chapter Two: Beggar Announces Arrival of Jesus to Pilate.......... 92
Chapter Three: Zebediah Reports to Zealots................................. 96
Chapter Four: Pilate and the Generals Confer............................... 98
Chapter Five: Kaiaphas Meets with Pilate.................................... 100
Chapter Six: Spy tells of Judas... 102
Chapter Seven: Moneychangers.. 104
Chapter Eight: Judas' Arrest 108

Chapter Nine: Judas Reports to Jesus...110
Chapter Ten: March Across Kidron Valley. Jesus' Arrest............113
Chapter Eleven: Judas Questioned After Arrest of Jesus 118
Chapter Twelve: Jesus at Sanhedrin 122
Chapter Thirteen: Judas' Death 131
Chapter Fourteen: Pilate hears Sanhedrin reports and sends
                    Jesus to Antipas 133
Chapter Fifteen: After Antipas 136
Chapter Sixteen: Jesus with Pilate... 139
Chapter Seventeen: Jesus—Second Visit to Pilate 142
Chapter Eighteen: Arimathea Goes to Pilate 144
Chapter Nineteen: Mary Magdalene at the Tomb 155
Chapter Twenty: Isaac and Nicodemus 157

Afterward 163

BOOK ONE

CHAPTER ONE

Early Pilgrimage to Jerusalem

MEMBERS OF THE FAMILY slowly began to awake and stir. The girls had begun to stretch and whine. They came out of the tent and washed their faces in the water from the bucket. Soon Mary, Joseph James, the younger boys, Cephas and his wife Yael and their babies, everyone, stretched and groaned. Mary, Yael and the older girls were cutting figs and brewing some herbal tea. Mounds of hummus and strips of pita were spread on the wagon lid for all to eat. Everyone sat or squatted around the fire, rubbing their eyes and stretching again. It was just after dawn, and the desert floor was chilly. The girls hugged and shivered. The men and boys loaded the wagon and the donkeys.

After the meal, the women went to pack up the loose items in the saddlebags as the men took down the tents. All the other families in the caravan were doing the same. It was still dangerous territory. Most of the families had come from the northern Galilee and had been escorted by some very dangerous-looking men riding horses—they were armed to the teeth, although the men had more weapons than teeth. Most wore rags around their faces to cover old scars, and avoid the sand in the winds. This was the beginning of the second day of the trip which took them through the rough and wild lower Galilee and past the Samaritan territory where they were not welcome. When all the families were packed and ready to move, the leader of the men gave the command and the line began to wind down the rough roadway.

Jesus and James were considered to be men of the family because they had already read from the torah as part of their Bar Mitzvah initiations and could walk along the wagon where their mother Mary rode with the girls. Joseph had gotten quite old and sick by this time, but insisted on filling his role as the head of the family and driving the ox cart. The other boys were permitted to walk with Jesus and James some of the time and the rest they rode in the cart with their sisters and the other women.

Jesus had begun early in the trip to pepper his father with questions about the trip. He had been educated by the local Pharisee priests who were opposed to sacrifice, and yet the family was going to the Temple for the express purpose of offering animals in sacrifice under the auspices of the Sadducee priests who controlled the temple and conducted the sacrifices. These priests were hereditary ministers who became wealthy controlling the temple sacrifices.

"But, father, what good is a dead animal to god?"

"It is our way. God has protected us and we must obey his commandments."

"Yes, yes. I know that. But he doesn't protect us. We are under the fist of the Romans, now, and the Assyrians before and the Babylonians before that. We are poor and must pay taxes to the Romans."

At this Mary broke in, "Don't complain about your poverty. Your father and his brother work very hard. They are tektons and so will you be. They do very well and are better off than most."

"I did not mean to complain about my lot, I mean the Jewish lot. What good has our being chosen done us now?"

"God's ways cannot be questioned. We might be punished because we have not been pious enough and observed his commandments."

"The only ones his commandments make better are the Sadducees. They get rich on these sacrifices and do little for us."

"Don't speak ill of the Sadducees."

"First, we know God told Abraham not to sacrifice Isaac. For us, that was the end of human sacrifice, which many of our neighbors do."

"Yes, but I don't get the idea. Why take a living thing and burn it to make God happy? He doesn't eat. I don't even know if he can smell."

"Good point. Many agree with you."

"I mean why take something of value and destroy it?"

"Alright. You made your point."

"I'm just thinking now. If someone else denies themselves something, like food or a wife, or something, how does that make them better in God's eyes?"

"Alright. We get it."

"If I sacrifice myself, how are other people made better?"

"Enough, Jesus."

"I'm just thinking out loud."

Jesus was getting to be like this now. Asking questions all day. Finally, Mary spoke up: "Jesus, leave your father alone. Go talk to James." James eagerly looked up, now he would have Jesus to himself while Jesus thought out loud.

"Rabbi Naimi does. He quotes Jeremiah who said 'What does God want smoke for?' Besides, God already said he didn't want sacrifices. Didn't he tell Abraham not to kill his son and sacrifice him to show his faith? Why would God want to have us lose something so that the fat Sadducees can have it? We should give to the poor or tithe to the church, but sacrifice a good animal up in smoke, it doesn't make sense."

"As you say, many people especially the ones who returned from Babylonia no longer sacrifice. That is something you can decide when you are the head of the family. But now, we sacrifice."

"Rabbi Naimi says the Sadducees are in a league with the Romans."

"Well, not exactly. They are stuck. The Sadducees have to keep the peace. They do what the Romans say but protect us from some of the bad things the Romans might do."

So the talk went on as the long line of families bumped down the gray dust of the countryside. Occasionally they would come to a well where the local clan owning the well would charge for the water drawn from it. The people would jump down and stretch their legs and groan, before climbing back for the rest of the journey.

When the clan had come to the area outlying Jerusalem, a loose line of men had assembled by the side of the road. As each family came up, the men would jostle for position and appeal to the head of the family to rent his campsite for the Passover holiday. Each would shout out the benefits of his side—water nearby, level ground, so many steps to the Temple, shade trees and the area. The head of the family would haggle with the men for the best price and then be lead off to the campsite. Joseph had selected a site he was familiar with west of the city—no water, no trees, but an hour's walk to the Temple. When they arrived, the family members all went about their duties to set up camp, start the fire, bed down the donkeys, and feed the children. Soon the sun began to set and the cool desert wind began to bring in some dust. The families lined up with their dishes around the bubbling pots of lentil soup and stew. Jesus and the older boys went off to their own circle and ate by themselves. They could not wait for the next morning.

At dawn, the camp began to stir again. Everyone had duties and went about them without hesitation or fuss. The breakfast figs and mare's milk were assembled on the wagons by the women. Everyone drifted over to the cooking area to warm up and eat the breakfast.

By the time they had finished, a line had already assembled leading down the road toward the city. Normally a population of 25,000 had now swollen to 250,000. People from all directions were swarming from their camps down the road.

First on the agenda would be the markets where the women would buy provisions for the weekend. The older boys went with them to carry the parcels home. The market today stretched for the entire length of the main street and filled many of the side streets as well. Among the food stalls, merchants sat with piles of goods available for the pilgrims. Spices, new robes, sandals, knives, jewelry, cosmetics, furs, scrolls—a dizzying display of goods—at each stall, the vendor would show his wares and attempt conversation with the passersby to lure them to his stall. The next few days for these vendors would decide whether it was a good year or a bad year. This was the best time to make money; by Monday, it would be over.

The pilgrims were jammed into narrow lanes as they squeezed through the crowds past each booth. It was exhausting. It was also easy to lose a child or two in the masses, so the cries back and forth between the women and their offspring mingled with the vendors hawking their wares.

Towards the afternoon, the men began to form the lines leading to the Court of the Temple where they could buy the animals to sacrifice. Jews and the Canaanites for miles around had such festivals where the priests would sacrifice animals to the respective deities. The Jews had followed the ceremonies of their neighbors for centuries and it was an endemic practice in every country on their particular feast days.

The men with fat purses would enter the battery of money changing tables. The changers had purchased their spots from the Temple priests and had piles of shekels in neat stacks in front of them. Today was their day to make their money for the year. Because the coins used in the empire often came from Rome and bore the image of Caesar, the coins, although necessary for commerce, were nonetheless idolatrous. They had the stamped profile of a ruler who insisted he be worshipped as a god. The coin was an idol by itself. The Temple authorities would not accept these pieces of moving idolatry and insisted on dealing in shekels—the special coinage of Jerusalem which bore images of mostly fruit or vines, but no humans. The exchange for the pilgrims was a costly but necessary transaction for the Passover sacrifice. Joseph and Cephas made their way through the lines around the money changers booths and made the exchange enough for an fine animal.

Further on, in the Court of Gentiles, there were huge pens of animals on display as the men passed by. The place stank. Thousands of calves, lambs, doves, chickens were bleating, squealing, chirping, squawking, groaning and urinating and defecating at every turn. Vendors stood before their pens shouting out their wares and prices. Layers of excrement covered the entire court from the days of loading the animals from the carts to the pens in the Temple. In front of each pen, pilgrims stood with their purses in hand haggling with the merchants over the weight and quality of the animals.

These animals were of the highest and purest quality and grown locally. The pilgrims could never afford to herd their own animals the long distance to Jerusalem, so they had to buy at exorbitant prices the local animals.

When Joseph, Cephas and the boys had picked out a decent lamb, he lead it off on a string to the next line—those waiting to have the priest sacrifice the animal. After an hour or so, they had made their way to the front of the line. The priests' assistants took the animal and the fee for the sacrifice. Twelve animals at a time were lead to individual stone headrests. The priests walked down a long line of animals slitting the throat of each. The animals were permitted to drop and bleed into gutters until they had bled out and were ready for the fire.

As each animal bled into a small pool, a priest would walk by and dip a cloth wrapped around a pole in the blood and daub the blood on the altar behind him. Two assistants would then walk down the line and grab each animal carcass and lift it onto a grate where a large fire was burning. As the animals began to sizzle and burn, the pilgrims were lead out of the room so that twelve more sets of pilgrims and their animals were ushered into the sacrifice area.

As Jesus and James descended the stairs from the sacrifice behind Joseph and Cephas, Jesus couldn't contain himself. "Father, is this the way they always do this?"

"Why, yes."

"But, I mean, the priests don't even look at you. You put your own money in the pot, they take your animal and they never say anything. They don't even look at you. They just mumble the prayers. And then we go."

"What did you expect?"

"Well, if this is a holy event...I mean it has no dignity, no character...It's just a...I mean we slaughter our animals with more care."

"But you knew them. You named them."

"These men are priests. They're supposed to be more...spiritual."

"Today, there are 250,000 people all wanting animals sacrificed. What did you expect? This is their busiest day of the year."

"And their most profitable. I could hardly hear the prayers. They were just mumbling. Does God really hear them, is this really for him? Why does he want this?"

"Jesus, we've always done this. For hundreds of years."

"Does God really want us to kill an animal and smell its smoke? I think it's a colossal waste."

"You're entitled to your opinion, but I think you've been listening too much to these Pharisees."

Jesus sunk into one of his deep contemplation modes on the way back to the camp. James knew not to disturb him when he was like this. Something was rumbling around in that head.

After the three days in Jerusalem, and three nights in a campsite the family had rented from a local landowner, the family started to pack up to leave. The women and girls bustled among the kitchen utensils, while the men rolled the tent and packed the saddlebags and gear. One of the men to ride along with the caravan rode up and began to give instructions to Joseph on where the return caravan would assemble. By mid-morning, everyone had been fed and the ox cart was packed. It was time to place the saddlebags on the donkeys. Suddenly, Mary yelled at James and the other boys.

"Jesus, where is Jesus? Is he lost?"

James, of course, knew where Jesus was. "He went down to the grove of trees near the Temple to debate with the men."

Mary turned to Joseph. "I'll have to go get him. Come, James, show me where." The two hustled down the road to the Temple.

After they entered the Susa gate, and went forward towards the Antonia Palace, the walls of the Temple became visible.

There were various scholars sitting in circles conducting sermons and lecturing on learned subjects. Normally, there would be a charge for attending put in a plate at the master's feet. However, there was a particularly large crowd standing around a group of the men. As Mary and James pressed through the crowd, they could see Jesus standing in front of the master and, as was his custom, peppering him with questions. Occasionally, the rest of the men chuckled as Jesus asked the master a particularly hard question.

Mary came up and grabbed Jesus by the arm. "Jesus, we are leaving today, why did you wander off?"

The crowd began to laugh at this smart young man being disciplined by his mother. "Oh, mother. Not now. Can't I stay a little longer?"

"No. We're all packed and it's time to leave."

One of the older men spoke up. "Madam, this boy has a gift, you must send him for more education."

Mary said, "His father is a tekton," she said with some pride. "He works in Sepphoris and this boy will be a very good one, too."

The rest of the men began to mumble. "Madam, that would be a waste, he would make a fine scholar or a rabbi."

"Well, we haven't time for that now." Mary dragged Jesus by the arm back to the family's campsite. "He has to earn a living."

CHAPTER TWO

Jesus Leaves Nazareth to Study

"JESUS, YOU CAN'T LEAVE like that. Where is your cloak and when will you be back? Cephas and the boys need you for the work in Tiberius. And what will you eat? And how about your appointment with Zvi; when will you be back for that?" Mary was not in a good mood and had two children clutching at her knees and following her around the house. "And I need your help here. What will I tell Cephas? He needs you."

"Oh please, Mother. You've known I've wanted to do this for weeks and now with the spring I can do it. I've told Cephas and he has no problem. He wanted me to take the donkey, but I don't want it. You've known about this, now leave me alone." Jesus was sixteen and had just completed his year with the Pharisee priests in Sepphoris. He had long announced his intention to become a priest and study Jewish law, but wanted to go to Jerusalem to attend the open air schools held by learned men around the Temple area.

For the past three years, since his Bar Mitzvah, he had been working with Cephas—his stepfather—on the contracting work necessary to rebuild the houses burned or destroyed by the Roman hunting parties who had sought out the leaders of the revolt and destroyed their homes, murdered the men and scattered the families. It was a booming business for the carpenters and masons to restore the houses throughout the Galilee. Joseph, his father, had been the leader

11

of the clan and assembled a crew of laborers, and carpenters to do the work, but his right hand man had been Cephas, his younger brother.

While the business was growing, the brothers could not afford a wife from a wealthy family; so Joseph had negotiated with Anne and Joachim, Mary's parents who were loathe to let her go to such a poor man, but Joachim had known Joseph and liked him, so they were married. Joseph's luck changed almost immediately, and the business grew. When Cephas wanted a wife, they could afford a decent bride price. Now the brothers began to produce sons to help them in the business. The eldest, Jesus, was a fine addition; he wasn't very strong, but he was excellent in the fine carpentry work needed for the cabinets and decorations in rich men's houses. His work brought a good price; but Jesus was unhappy. From the earliest, he had been sent to the Pharisee priests in town. Four days a week he and James went to school and studied the torah, the mishnah and learned to analyze the stories and arguments for debate with the priests. For his good work, and after much pleading on his part, he was also sent for one day to the old retired scribe who took in a few students in greek and latin literature. After a while, he took his brother James to the classes and helped him with his lessons. James adored Jesus and was overjoyed to follow him wherever he went.

All was going well for the extended family which lived together in a series of buildings and additions at the edge of town. They ate communal meals and observed all the Jewish rituals. In the wild hills of Galilee, they were indeed becoming a family to be admired. And then Joseph fell ill. He lingered on his deathbed for several months losing weight, eating less and slowly wasting away. When he died, Cephas was overwrought. The brothers had been close, but it was more a fear of assuming the leadership of the clan and the contracting business.

Mary came to him while Cephas sat staring off into space and immobile with fear. His wife Yael was a pretty young girl but no help. When Mary came to him, she had four sons and her daughters and was now 26. Although Cephas was now the head of the family, everyone looked to Mary for guidance.

"Cephas...Cephas. Look at me... You must listen... Now pay attention. You must get the crew ready for tomorrow's work. And then there is the account to collect from the job at the Rahar complex. It is overdue… Cephas…are you listening?"

"Yes…Yes I am. I know…I know." Cephas had always been a bit cowed by Mary who was the matriarch of the clan ever since he, Joseph and Mary had moved into their house. She had ordered Yael, Cephas' wife, around and run the family while the men were away on their various jobs.

But Mary was a force he could not deny. She pushed and prodded him as she began to assume the role of a matriarch. Even with the children at her knees, she organized the crews and pushed Cephas through his schedule while Yael tagged along at her heels and helped with the hearth and the children.

Mary's weakness was Jesus. Her bright little boy—a scholar. He was to be permitted to leave the carpentry business and study. In the village, the highest attainment a Jewish male could reach was to be a scholar, not a soldier, not an athlete, but a scholar. Jesus had answered her prayers and was a scholar—Torah, Mishnah, Greek, Latin. He no longer spoke with much of a Galilean accent. His speech was scholarly, correct. And he could talk… In the debates with his Pharisee teachers, he could propound theories and analyze texts. They recommended Jerusalem, to study with the brightest and best. After much discussion, Cephas had agreed to release him from the work crew because he too recognized his ability. James had even started to pester everyone about becoming a scholar. No. The time had come for Jesus to leave, but not James.

But, out of the blue, Jesus announced he wanted to go first into the wilderness to think. What was he thinking? Mary had worked hard to get Cephas to release Jesus to study in Jerusalem and now he wanted more time off. To do what? To think? Alone? With all the Roman raiding parties in the hills? And without his cloak?

"Mother, I don't have time for this? My life is moving so fast, I have to think things through. In the bible, all the great men spent time in the wilderness and received their calling. I'll be back before Passover."

"Where will you go? Where can we reach you?"

"I'll be fine."

Eventually, she had to let him go. He slowly disappeared over the gray hills on the road to the east and the wilderness of the gray hills.

CHAPTER THREE

Judas and Jesus in Judas' Home; Early Travels

I T WAS EARLY AFTERNOON, Judas and Jesus walked from the Temple along the streets of the upper city where the nicer homes spread west. The streets were nicely paved and planters of desert flowers were tucked neatly against the front of each entrance way. On the paving before each doorway, there were mosaics with decorative patterns and the house numbers. Judas was well-dressed as a young business man and scribe. Jesus looked like the dusty road-weary traveler he was. He had already begun to dress like a Nazorite and had not cut his hair for several years now. In his travels, it had grown dusty and matted. He wore the linen caftan adopted by the very religious who vowed to wear clothes made only from plants. His was a rough brown linen, but ragged and worn. The contrast between the two young men drew stares from the nosy neighbors passing the two, especially in the upper city. Jesus and Judas talked excitedly and were oblivious to their surroundings. Jesus had begun to tell Judas of his trip to Egypt where he had studied at the large Temple of Alexandria. Egypt was more free of Roman oppression and the Jews were a minority there; but the Jewish community was quite prosperous and enjoyed religious freedom. Jesus was expressing how surprised he was by their reliance on the newer influence of Greek civilization sweeping through the Egyptian community. Judas was astonished at how the Egyptian Jews had been lured into some of the Greek influences which now consumed Egyptian society.

"How can a people believe in gods who lie, cheat, steal, practice adultery? How can they respect them? Their gods are an abomination. How can they believe such a one who would beget bastards by their human worshippers?"

"It's not quite so simple. This Plato and Socrates do not seem influenced by the theology. But their reasoning and deductions are sound. They seem to develop moral conclusions by sheer reasoning out of their heads and hearts. Spinning out of themselves like spiders, they construct beautiful webs. We Jews observe and research to construct our laws from the Torah and put one law on top of another like building stones. We are more like bees, we collect from the flowers and turn it into honey. They have a philosopher who does the same — Aristotle. I am still unsure of their meaning. I have been letting it sift in my head to see what it all means. I'm beginning to believe that Jews should take the law into their hearts rather than relying on an analysis of the meaning of the law, and reason more like Plato."

By this time, the two had come to Judas' family home; the twilight was fading and the streets were filled with people rushing home for the Sabbath meal. Judas kissed the mezuzah on the door and entered. "Mom, I'm home. I've brought a guest."

His mother came out with the scarf over her head for the blessing over the candles. As she saw Jesus, she stopped and gaped. "Mom, this is Jesus. You remember him from before."

In front of the woman stood Jesus, a dusty dirty unkempt ragamuffin redolent of many scents — none of which were particularly pleasant. Catching herself, and bringing back her well-bred demeanor, she managed to stammer, "Of course, of course. Well, you're most welcome. Come in, please."

She turned to Judas. "You must go to the Mikveh and take your bath. We will go to the service soon." She shot a stern glance at Judas. "And lend him a robe, Judas. He looks like he needs some freshening up."

"Yes, mother." Judas turned to Jesus with apologetic shrug. "Come on, Jesus. You get the picture."

Jesus nodded in good humor. "Thank you, ma'am. Thank you for your hospitality. The house looks lovely, especially the new mural."

The woman melted. The educated tones—even with the slight Galilean accent—were soft and strong. Yes, this was Judas' old friend from several years ago. Well, he certainly had changed. That smell, and that Nazorite hair—like a wild animal. What was he doing? But, a very nice young man. Yes, she remembered. The sparkling bright eyes, the brilliant white teeth and the calm, sensitive manner. She remembered now.

The two left and went to the family's private mikveh. Judas was chuckling and clucked conspiratorially at Jesus. "You almost threw the old girl off her camel. She thought you were here to rob us. I saw her counting the silver."

"Now, now! She was very nice and never lost her composure, although she must have thought I would eat her young."

The men stripped and slowly immersed in the cool water. Always, the mikveh cleansed the body and the mind. As they sat silently up to their eyes in the water and were quiet. Slowly, the cares and frets they had carried fell from their brows as their heartbeats slowed and the Sabbath rest began. After they were finished, Jesus was handed Judas' robe and sandals. Judas' mother had already taken Jesus' clothes and put them in a box for the temple poor.

"Never mind, you are one of my boys. I can't have you looking like that. Enjoy."

With everyone fresh from the mikveh and in their Sabbath robes, the family and Jesus went to the local synagogue for services. This was a big social event. As the families filed into the open air foyer, it was time to meet and discuss the affairs of the day. It was also time to look over and evaluate your neighbors. Was he getting fat? Was she going gray? Was this man's new wife appropriate, she looked like a floozy. Were their robes in the latest fashion? And the teenagers mingled. The younger males hooted, chased each other and punched their friends in the shoulders. The younger females huddled closely and exchanged gossip and secrets. The older teenagers were shyly beginning to talk boy-girl with minimal eye contact and much drawing designs in the dust with their feet.

Eventually, the shamus opened the doors and everyone filed into the pews. The women went to the second floor and could look through latticework at the bimah below. The men sat in a semi-circle surrounding the bimah. Simeon, Judas and Jesus were in the back row—but Jesus drew a good bit of attention, even washed up and hair combed. His long hair and beard spoke of a holy man—a Nazorite from Galilee. In this respectable community, he was an oddity.

The service followed the time-honored formula. The 18 prayers, the torah section and the sermon. This sermon was a rather dry scholarly piece debating an obscure point interpreting the torah section. Soon the service was over.

The families all filed out of the synagogue and began to separate on their way to their homes. Judith and Simeon walked ahead with Jesus and Judas following, and then Judas' sisters. When they reached the home, the Sabbath meal was all laid out so that Judith and the girls would not work on what was now the Sabbath.

The family sat around the dinner table where the plates of food had already been laid out. The family assembled around the table which had been set before the services.

Judas' father turned to Judas, full of pride. "Tell Jesus what you are doing."

Judas rolled his eyes. "Father, he is not interested."

"No, no. Tell him."

"Well, my father has arranged for me to be placed with a large mercantile house as a clerk so that I can learn the business."

"Ah." Jesus nodded respectfully.

"But father, listen to Jesus. He has interesting news about Egypt."

"All right, Jesus. Tell us."

"I have returned from a very interesting journey. The Jews in Alexandria do very well. They do not suffer the outrages of the Romans who seem more concerned about controlling the Egyptians and leave the Jews alone." As Jesus spoke, he had an intense and serious air about him. Something would not let Judas and his family take their eyes off him.

He was thin, but muscular. He was not a city dweller, he had the rough ambling walk of a laborer. Judas' sisters, approaching marital age in their early teens, examined him closely to see if their parents might approve of him. Already, their father had, not too subtly, been bringing young single business associates around. Most of them were a little too plump, a little too fussy or not interesting enough. Jesus was young, and had an air of mystery about him; but he had no prospects, or so it seemed. The life of those wandering scholars was not easy; often, they would teach the schools where the young men prepared for their Bar Mitzvahs as a melamed or sometimes they preached at the local synagogues in hopes of getting a study group together. More often than not, they just studied. Their parents would not want that life for them; but still this Jesus had a magnetism and he was their revered older brother's friend.

Jesus sat near the head of the table between Simeon and Judas.

"Madam, this looks wonderful!" Jesus could not help exclaiming.

"Enjoy yourself. It is a blessing." Judith had prepared the usual Sabbath meal, but to Jesus, it was a feast. As the platters were passed, he heaped his plate full and could not restrain his appetite. The fruits, the chicken legs, the hummus, the honey and jams. The family ate sparingly, but was amused as Jesus gobbled everything. The sisters could not help giggling every time Jesus reached for another plate.

"It's been a long time since I ate like this. I've been traveling for quite a long time. I'm sorry. It's so good."

Judith was beaming. "Eat, son, eat. You do me honor."

"Then, you must tell us where you have been," Simeon said.

"As Judas knows, my father was a tekton in a small village near Sepphoris and I worked on his crew repairing the houses and buildings there. When he died, my uncle Cephas who had worked with my father and I continued to pursue the business. But I was too restless, so I wandered the world stopping in the cities to seek out the great scholars. I could always join a tekton crew or teach at the synagogues to pay my way. I have been to Athens, Rome, Carthage, Persia, and studied their ways. At this point, I am a little confused and happy to return to Jerusalem to sort things out in my head. I have just come from Elephantine where the Jews have a large school, and a big community."

"Judas, how did you meet Jesus?" asked Judith. On hearing that Jesus could be a tekton, her interests had picked up. He did have some prospects—a good builder with a decent crew could take care of a family very nicely. It was not as prestigious as a scribe, but Jesus with all his studies, could certainly hold his own at the Temple discussions and be a pillar of the community.

"I met Jesus several years ago when he came down to the Temple to hear the scholars talk. We had many long discussions and shared many ideas."

"Yes, that was when I first started on my travels."

"I visited the Temple in Alexandria."

Judas' father broke in. "They have a Temple in Egypt? Why, isn't that forbidden? Only the Temple in Jerusalem is permitted."

"Well, yes that is true. The wealthy jews and the main body of people do look to Jerusalem as the center of our religion, but there is a controversy. Many jews see the Sadducees in Jerusalem as corrupt and controlled by Rome. It seems Rome permits the Herods to control the appointment of the chief priests and they care little for the people. So a large group of people look to the Temple in Alexandria for guidance. It is run by true Zadokite priests, without the pure hereditary lines, but extremely zealous of the law. They live lives of simplicity and don't flaunt wealth as the Sadducees do, a number of zealots…"

"Whoa. Wait a minute. There are zealots in Alexandria?" Judas' father burst out. "They are a problem here. They stir up the Romans."

As Jesus spoke, he looked each person at the table directly in the eye and made a personal contact with each. His gentle handsome face, flashing eyes and personal enthusiasm electrified each family member. As he looked into the eyes of Judas' sisters, they could only melt and giggle shyly. Jesus was an exotic personage to them, unlike the well-bred, well dressed but bland men of Jerusalem from whom they were expected to have a husband. Jesus sent ripples of excitement through the core of these young teenage girls. Judas the older brother was of course amused by the effect Jesus was having on his sisters who only recently had reached puberty.

As the evening meal was cleared away, Jesus and Judas went up to the roof to talk quietly in the cool night air. Jesus began to discuss the politics of the time—which were a bewildering array of sects and factions. Judas was always the practical realist who was feeling restless in his relatively comfortable world in the sophisticated middle class world of Jerusalem. He sought a life of action and wanted to rid the country of this Roman oppression. Jesus was ever the idealist. He enjoyed both study and teaching of the deeper meanings. He felt the Jews needed a reeducation and reform to the purer forms of religious life, but he hadn't quite figured out how. If they had a deeper feel for their religion, they might band together more easily and oppose the Romans.

Jesus described how the greek followers of Plato and Socrates had begun to examine a means by which human beings would be trained to examine within themselves a natural morality. This differed from the Jews who over 1000 years had slowly built a system of laws and commentaries which enabled them to regulate and enrich their communities. The Torah had a large collection of moral tales which were their own history as they developed as a nation and in their relationship to God. The mishnah collected over 600 years of debates over the meaning of the Torah. The men all studied this in their adolescence and continued to debate for the rest of their lives.

The Jews as well as the Greek platonic followers endlessly debated and examined the meaning of human behavior, but from different perspectives. To Jesus, the similarity and differences were fascinating and something he was grasping to reconcile. His visit to Alexandria was the ultimate opportunity to see the two side by side. Alexandria at the time was the most exciting center of intellectual thought of the Greek civilization and joined the intellectual Greek life with the vitality and mystery of the Egyptian. Outside of Jerusalem, Alexandria was a center for sophisticated Jewish life. The two influences provided a heady inspiration for the wandering student Jesus had become. Judas listened, rapt, to his descriptions til the early morning hours.

As Jesus prepared to leave the next day, Judas his mother and sisters saw him to the door. "Well, where to now, Jesus?"

"I will go see my mother and family up north, and then I would like to spend some time with the Essenes."

"I would love to go with you. They have a community not far from here. Could you stop by and see me before you go?"

"Of course. I should be back in a few weeks."

As Jesus left, he could hear the beginnings of the argument between Judas and his parents about leaving the prestigious mercantile house in which he had been accepted as a junior scribe to idle away his time in some remote Essene village.

CHAPTER FOUR

Jesus and Judas Meet Essenes

IT WAS EARLY EVENING when Jesus knocked on the door of Judas' father. Judas' mother came to the door. "Why, Jesus, how nice to see you again." Jesus was a favorite guest of the house; he and Judas had been friends for many years. Judas was in his father's office just off the doorway facing the street. He had completed his apprenticeship in a large mercantile house, and now worked with his father.

"Jesus. What brings you by this time?"

"The Essenes. We must visit the Essenes." Jesus was referring to a sect of Jews who practiced a form of monastic Judaism. They had communities in many of the Jewish cities as well as a few complexes of their own out in the wilderness areas. Jesus' enthusiasm over new ideas was always captivating and Judas, as one of his close friends, could never resist being swept up in the lure.

"Which one and where?" Judas, of course, had heard of this group but they were rather secretive and kept themselves aloof from ordinary Jewish life—even their communes in Jerusalem.

"They practice a form of Judaism that seems to look for some messiah in the future who will usher in a golden age. They are heavy in ritual and live a very strict lifestyle. They often invite potential converts to their communes and I have gotten a pass for the one out in Qumram. What do you say?"

Judas was dressed in the fine urban clothing as befitted the son of a scribe in the city of Jerusalem. He wore a tunic of bright white cotton with a blue and silver border. He had fine sandals laced up to the knee. His hair was oiled and hung in fine curls from his brow. He mind was cluttered with the details of his business. He stood open-mouthed as he looked at Jesus and began to consider slipping away on his newest venture.

"Wait here," Judas said, edging to the office his father occupied. He knew it would be difficult to leave his father once again. He had been taking time to engage in a number of undercover operations with the sicarii. His father certainly did not approve of any of that rebellious organization, and seemed content with the status quo under Roman rule, but Judas had a fever in his blood. He enjoyed the dual life he had been leading—slipping from his father's contented security of the business world in Jerusalem to the rough company of the sicarii who attacked Jews collaborating with the Romans or the occasional Roman who strayed from the safety of the Roman legions stationed at Antonia Palace in the center of Jerusalem. But Jesus was a different matter. Jesus awakened in Judas a thirst for knowledge and self-discovery. Jesus' travels had taken him to the world's cities where he sought to discover the other cultures. Of course, he could always stay in the Jewish enclaves since in virtually every major city, Jews had dispersed to conduct trade or practice skills unknown or not well cultivated in those countries. Over half of the Jewish population lived outside Judea and practiced such trades as medicine, gold, silver or copper crafts, poetry and drama, and traded in exotic goods of all sorts. After a brief visit to the local synagogue, Jesus was welcome in some members' home with his stories of travel in other lands. For Judas to join Jesus now in another of his adventures was a joy he could not pass up. Besides the Essenes were a mystery—known to exist but their rites and practices were still a mystery to the uninitiated. And it was just over a day's walk from Jerusalem.

After Judas extricated himself from his father's admonishments and his mother's warnings and fear, he and Jesus packed some supplies and took off for Qumram.

Judas and Jesus were met at the gate to the Essene community and taken to an adjacent small room. Three of the men began to interrogate them intensely. Judas had thought to bring with him letters from several of the Temple authorities vouching for his good faith. He held in reserve his letters from sicarii chieftans. Jesus of course had nothing. As they began to question them further, they were asked specific questions of Jewish history and law. Because of their ample prior training, both men were able to convince the interrogators that they were not merely curiosity seekers, or worse, spies, but serious students of Jewish heritage they were admitted. They were given the iconic pure white caftans of the community and shown to beds in the long structure. Since it was close to dinnertime as they arrived, they quickly joined the line outside the refectory in an elaborate hand washing ritual and took their places on the benches at the periphery of the tables.

For almost the entire week, no one spoke to them except to direct them to their duties in the community of feeding the animals and cleaning the area. All buildings were maintained in a pristine white which was almost blinding in the desert sun. The men—there were no women in this section—wore also blinding white caftans. It was explained that men were permitted to marry but communication among the sexes was extremely limited to certain times of the year. Their rules for marriage and times of sex were severely circumscribed. As explained, those rules were complex and confusing; but, somehow the community did produce a small number of children over in the women's sector.

Each day there were periods of extensive rituals and prayers signaled by a bell at regular intervals. Dietary laws, ritual purity laws and even obscure rules from the Torah were scrupulously observed. This stultifying regimen was beginning to wear on Jesus and Judas during their first week until the sermon during the Sabbath.

A figure called only the Teacher of Righteousness was invoked as the leader of the community. It was difficult to determine whether this was the one preaching or a legendary character. However, from the gist of the sermon, this figure would bring forth an age of righteousness which would free the Jewish people from repression and usher in an age of justice. In this age, the wicked would be punished. Although Jesus had always thought that the Pharisees were the most insistent on strict observance of the laws and required rituals, they were condemned as "lover of smooth things," who sought only excessive ritualism but not the kingdom of God. They were considered to be hypocrites. This meant they were willing to accept the status quo with Roman rule and not rigorously pursue the strict observance of Jewish law as a form of salvation for all people. The speaker referred to the wicked as both some controlling foreign power as well as those collaborating with it. They envisioned a "war" meaning a struggle of 40 years when those of the community led by the Teacher of Righteousness would cause the Jewish community to reject their lax ways and begin to undermine "the wicked."

It began to be clear to Jesus that this sermon was advocating a non-violent reformation of the entire Jewish religion including the destruction of those who controlled the Temple and misled the people while collaborating with Rome. From their tone and extensive religious training, Jesus could see that these so-called Essenes or as they styled themselves—the Poor—were young Zadokite priests, whose particular disdain was directed at their superiors, those holding hereditary positions in the Temple hierarchy.

These men had been trained in the Sadducee tradition in all the rituals and practices of the Temple, but had grown to hate the wealthy dynastic cult of priests who by dint of inheritance acceded to the upper levels of the Temple priesthood. This strangling control of the Jews and Jewish religion was seen as the main evil interfering with the pursuit of Jewish independence and a world of justice and righteousness. By controlling this cowardly but greedy priesthood, the Romans were able to control not only the religion but the Jewish courts, hereditary rights, commercial rules and in general all Jewish social life. They sought the overthrow of the Sadducee Temple structure. Unfortunately, it would result, as foretold, in the martyrdom of the Teacher of Righteousness in the process.

Following the sermon, as Jesus was wont to do, he went to a quiet corner of the community and stared out across the wasteland, lost in his thoughts. Judas, as many of those who knew Jesus, knew better than to interrupt this trancelike state of thought and meditation. Clearly, he had been moved by the thoughts of these young Sadducee rebels who sought their own version of salvation. He was trying to fit the vision of the Essenes into his own.

Somehow, somewhere, this visit to the Essenes was nagging at him with some answer, some clue. Certainly, the Righteous Teacher who was the inspiration for their community had something to do with it. In ages past, the Jewish tribes had produced wise men inspired by God to lead the Jews out of their misery and let them survive. Moses—an adopted Egyptian prince had been reached by God. The Judges—Samuel, Eli, and Nathan had all been reached by God to find the devout but strong secular leader. The Prophets had always advocated repentance and devotion to Torah. In each age, devout men had arisen, inspired by God, to save the Jews.

But these Essenes. They could not be the answer. They had run away from confrontation, they had secreted themselves in a lonely stretch of desert. They observed strange and probably useless rituals. They could not be the answer.

But who could overcome the Romans? They were the sole superpower in the world, immensely powerful. Roman legions had the greatest power the world had ever known. Yet they had no soul. Their gods were a laughable bunch of greedy raunchy, brutal animals—how could they inspire? They had trampled on the gifts of philosophy, democracy, drama, song, and poetry the Greeks had given them. Surely, God did not intend for them to survive. Within their beings they bore the cause of their own destruction, inspired by their own gods.

Somehow, the Essenes, these monastic men in gleaming white robes with their absurd rituals meant something. Certainly discipline. But what else? They sought to undermine the very underpinnings of the Jewish religion by contesting the authority of the wealthy dynastic Sadducees who controlled the Temple. With their stranglehold on the ritual of sacrifice, controlling the center of religious life and their disgusting accommodation with the Romans, they doomed the people to a life of subservience, poverty and eventually annihilation. The real enemies of the Jewish people were the very priests who held the power. To bring in the true Kingdom of God as they foresaw, they sought to do away with the very Temple and the very priests who insidiously afflicted their own people. Somehow, someway, some man of insight and inspiration must reorganize the very foundation of the Jewish religion.

Slowly, Jesus arose and came over to Judas sat chewing idly on a desert weed. "Ah, back in the land of the living," Judas ventured, looking carefully up into his friend's eyes.

"Yes. Yes. It has been a good day. I think I have found something."

CHAPTER FIVE

Judas as Sicarii

THE PASS TOOK PLACE in the blink of an eye. The plump Egyptian woman with heavy kohl around her eyes handed the spice seller a scrap of leaf with the number 6 on it in the filthy port streets of Jaffa. She waddled swiftly on her way shouldering through the crowd. Along the way the narrow street had lines of men and women selling their wares. Boxes of fish, rabbits, pigs, goat meat hung from hooks, heaps of vegetables, open bags of grain, and everyone yelling their prices and products. The street had loose stones and mud and puddles of animal blood, dirty water. And the smells— in the beginning of the summer heat—the cauldron of close fetid aromas swirled in dizzying clouds from stand to stand. And the spice seller sat in front of 32 neat sacks of spices—kumin, saffron, lavender, frankincense were arranged in conical piles within the bags. In front of him were gleaming bronze scoops arranged around a scale. This was a port city and all manner of people filtered through—Egyptians, Phoenicians, Berbers, Nubians, Thracians, and each wore the dress of their land and spoke a myriad of languages. And the spice seller sat calmly at his low table and watched as the crowds and aromas swept past.

He was an old Egyptian with one eye missing, he wore the short kilt of Egyptians and sat cross-legged on the low stool. His head scarf was pulled low over his forehead to conceal the scar that ran from his scalp through his eye.

He remained immobile staring straight ahead as the Roman soldiers marched by. As they came the crowd parted to let them pass two abreast through the market. Dressed in full hardened leather armor and red kilts with plumed helmets, the ten men followed their Decion in step.

It wasn't until nearly three in the afternoon that Judas and Simon passed the spice seller's stand. Both wore the rough head scarfs of the desert berbers and made eye contact with no one. Until they stopped in front of the low table of spices. The spice seller broke the silence.

"I have some fresh kumin," he said in the Egyptian of Alexandria.

"How much will a shekel buy?" Judas asked in aramaic.

"2."

"Done."

Without more, the spice seller wrapped the spice in leaf and calmly put the scrap of leaf from the plump Egyptian woman in the mix and handed it to them. The price actually paid for a scoop of kumin was exorbitant and bore no relation to the figure quoted, but included the considerable fee for passing the scrap of leaf seamlessly and calmly to Judas.

The spice seller as a youth had fought the Romans as a guerilla warrior until he had received the sword blow to his head which left him without an eye and a tremor in his right side. The Jews had saved him in the battle, had tended to his injuries from the six months while he lay nearly lifeless on the cot of an old stable. Eventually they trained him as a zealot and installed him in Jaffa as the eyes, or more accurately the eye, and ears of the Egyptian community. He only knew Judas and Simon of the zealots and reported only to them; but he lived in the Egyptian neighborhood near the docks and kept an ear open for all things of interest to the zealots.

Judas picked up the rolled leaf and casually threw it into his sack. Judas was known as Iscariot because, concealed under his cloak, was a sicarius—a long dagger wrapped in leather. Simon, sometimes known as Magus, but also known as Zelotes, was in Jaffa to meet with Judas and was accompanying him to the small suite of rooms the zealots kept in the area where the Jewish area mingled with the Greek one.

The zealots were a group of loosely affiliated bands of guerilla warriors who repeatedly harassed and embarrassed the Romans, and the Jews who supported the Roman occupation. Occasionally it was difficult or unwise to kill or attack the Romans themselves because it could bring ugly reprisals from the brutal Roman consuls. As late as last year, a group of Samaritans, an ethnic group loosely affiliated with the Jews, had been caught and they were rounded up and brutally slaughtered in front of their village for some affront to the Pax Romana.

The Roman occupation followed the long established prescription for governing a conquered land—intimidation. With relatively few soldiers, the Romans could terrorize an entire city or countryside. The consuls were quick to seek out an example and deliver swift and overwhelming strikes at the community where the threat to Roman rule had occurred. In return, the Romans permitted the indigenous population to rule itself by its own governors and court system. Only crimes directly against the Roman peace, Pax Romana, were punished by Roman authorities. And many theft, rape, assaults were handled by local magistrates. Business, marital and civil wrongs were also dealt with by the indigenous authorities. And Judea was no exception. The Jews had governed themselves for over a thousand years and developed a sophisticated and complex series of written laws and commentaries which they used as precedent to follow. In fact, the Jews called themselves and were known as the people of the word—because they leaned heavily on the written word to guide them in their daily affairs. Going back to the torah, and their oral and written commentaries on the torah going back over 1000 years, the Jews had been and were continuing to develop a series of comments compiled in vast numbers of scrolls and carefully replicated by trained scribes of the rulings and discussions of their learned men and their judges, prophets and other wise men.

The Romans in order to control the population were able through subtle and not so subtle means to use the country's own institutions against the populace. And sadly, the most corrupted among the Jews was their own priesthood—the Sadducees.

Zadok in the days of Moses was designated a high priest. His descendants assumed the role of priests in hereditary fashion down to this day. As the twelve brothers of Joseph had divided themselves into the twelve tribes of Israel, the descendants of Zadok were assigned among them as their priests and religious leaders. As such they became a hereditary group scattered throughout the tribes for over 1000 years. They performed the religious rites of marriage, circumcision, funerals, the Sabbath and most important the animal sacrifices. As the language changed they became known as the Sadducees derived from the name of Zadok. Because the Jewish laws were often administered by the priests, Jews honored them with substantial fees for each sacrament and the buying and sacrificing of animals—doves, sheep and others of a particular refinement and purity. The Sadducees in blessing the sellers of the sheep and doves received considerable livelihood. Over the centuries, they became, at best, a wealthy, aristocratic and extremely learned extended family spread through the nation of Israel. Their respect and authority bridged inter-tribal, or territorial disputes and survived many different rulers.

It was this group the Romans were able to influence and control the most successfully. In return for not disturbing their historical and lucrative role as the designated priest class of the nation, the Romans insisted on naming the leader of the Sadducees High Priest of the Temple from among them and controlling his activities. Feeling a relative sense of prosperity and security throughout the Roman controlled territories, the Sadducees felt, if their role and standing were not threatened, they could inure themselves to the occasional Roman demand and conduct their business as usual. In fact, they became strong instruments to establish Roman control.

There were many who enjoyed considerable prosperity under the Romans. They employed many and gave business to many. But high on the list were the tax collectors. Roman occupation was a smoothly run and long successful enterprise which yielded necessary income to Rome and its nobility, but along the way many people siphoned off the stream. The most benefited class were the Procurators—whose appointment was an immensely lucrative opportunity to amass wealth with little control from Rome. Their minions, the tax collectors, were not Roman; they were indigenous people charged with the duty to exact Roman tribute and they did very well in the process. Of course, they were hated and reviled by the people.

It was the zealots and the sicarii who look on the responsibility of discouraging and undermining collaboration among the Jews with the Roman occupation. But tonight it would be a Roman soldier who felt the sting of those forces, at other times, it would be the tax collector, or the Roman spy.

In their apartment, Judas slowly shook the package of kumin on the table until the spice leaf fell. The number 6 on the spice leaf came from the Egyptian madam—a greedy woman who was only too happy to take Jewish shekels for an occasional piece of information. Pillow talk was common at her brothel, especially when fueled with strong wine. After satisfaction in the arms of her Egyptian beauties, men loved to talk and especially brag when appropriately comfitted by the houris. All kinds of information—family secrets, financial dealings, infidelities. It was a veritable feast of subjects. And Judas paid well.

Without another word, Judas and Simon hurried to the brothel.

"What is a soldier worth?" The sweating fat woman with kohl running in streams down her cheeks from her eyes on this hot day.

"How good is the information?"

"A liberty. A hundred released for liberty and some have come by to arrange for my girls."

"How high in rank?"

"The centurion and two others."

"Ah good! But you must separate them. The centurion must leave alone."

"Don't worry. If you help me, the other two will leave long after with big smiles."

"And drink. Do you have wine or that Egyptian beer?"

"Do you have to ask? I know the business."

"You have done well. Five shekels now, five shekels tomorrow."

This was a very fine price indeed. She could buy another fine slave for that sum alone. And one more slave, another source of income for fat Indira.

With the coins in her hand, she waited for the men to leave so she could put it in her secret cache.

"The legion will release men about the six and they'll be here about an hour."

"We'll be on the lookout."

Simon and Judas went out into the crowded streets of the port quarter.

Judas, Simon and the other sicarii mingled separately in the market streets, occasionally passing the doorway of the Egyptian brothel to see whether the Roman soldiers had come by yet. As the evening began to get dark, several men in Roman battle dress began to swagger down the narrow street. There were six of them, five foot soldiers and a centurion. They walked through the door and were offered a goblet of strong wine. Judas and the others made themselves invisible as they passed back and forth in the surrounding streets, killing time and keeping their eyes on the other passersby who might be guards or lookouts. After some time, the noise from the brothel became raucous and loud laughter could be heard. Eventually, the men began to emerge staggering and shouting, some were draped in the women's scarves and sang a bawdy lyric. The centurion and two men went off to another bar, the other three headed back to the barracks. A few hand signals by Judas directed the others to follow the centurion's crew. Judas and the others circled through a few alleys and were able to catch up to their prey at the rear of a warehouse along the docks.

Then they struck with the speed of a jaguar. The three Romans were caught from behind and their throats slit before they knew what hit them. They were then stabbed in the upper chest and dragged into an alley. There, they were stripped. Roman uniforms and weapons were always useful to the Zealots.

The next morning as the denizens of the lower city began to make their way on their daily routes, the three Romans were laying on their backs against the fountain in the middle of the square. All were naked except their plumed helmets and were covered in blood from the wounds to their necks and chests. On each chest in blood daubed from their wounds was the Hebrew letter "S" in case anyone doubted who was responsible. In case there was any further doubt, the men had all been circumcised—albeit a bit belatedly.

CHAPTER SIX

John the Baptist

A LARGE GATHERING SAT randomly along the banks of the Jordan river. The small, muddy river—hardly a river—was about thirty feet wide and spilled over rocks at the edge. The banks were green and the sun was warm and brilliant. Some people were drying off and eating their lunches. Some had piled their robes neatly along the bank in the vacant areas and were making their way down to form a line. Numerous assistants were guiding them by now in a long, irregular line as it curved down to the river's edge. As the crowd passed each assistant, he would utter a blessing in low tones as they passed and the people in line would respond with a prayer of their own. The scene was quiet and subdued.

The leader in each line would cross over several rocks aided by the assistants until they reached an area where they could step into the water about two feet deep and wade slowly till they were up to their waists in the water. Here, surrounded by assistants, the wader would meet a tall, impressive figure who would issue a blessing and beckon them over. The figure, John, was quite tall and very thin. He was wearing only a loin cloth as he stood in the water. His hair was a wild assortment of curls with drops of water clinging to them. With the sun striking the drops of water, he seemed to sparkle from behind with an aura of many colors. His bony forehead shone with beads of sweat and water. But his eyes were the most striking. Deeply inset under an overhanging brow, his eyes flashed and pierced each penitent as they waded up to him. He seemed to engage in a brief, silent exchange of thoughts as each person came forward. Then, aided by his assistants, the person would bend his knees and bend at the waist as he ducked beneath the river surface. He would rise up quickly and shake the water from his face. The assistants would guide the baptized back to shore over the rocks. As people were finished, they would congregate in a clearing on top of the hill overlooking the river.

Immersion in water in one form or another had been a part of religions for many centuries and in many areas. The area around Jerusalem from west of Egypt to past the Persia empire was always in need of rain, and water was a luxury. The richest cities sat near rivers, and bathing everywhere was a rare treat. The feeling of cleanliness, as fresh water washed away the grime and oils from the body, was a wonderful bracing shock to the system for all the peoples of the world.

Jews had celebrated ritual baths called mikvehs before the Sabbath and holy days for centuries. It was especially important for the rites of purification for women after their menstrual cycles. Water was with the sun as one of the most glorified elements of nature. The mikveh or ritual bath was as much a part of the week cycle as the Sabbath and gave a structure to the whole week.

John, however, took the ritual and used it as the center for his ministry. He had taken a vow of poverty and was well respected for this discipline. It was well known that he ate honey and locusts and wore only camel hair skins. But his personality overshadowed all. His intensity and fervor made his entire body shake, and all around him were overcome by the feeling. When he spoke, every ear was turned to his message.

As he ascended the slope from the river to address the crowd gathered after their baptisms, a silence fell. The air almost vibrated with silence. But, as frequently happened, an assistant of his gave the address.

Being an assistant of John was no easy task. He was now renowned throughout both Israel and Judea. Of course, he was a great preacher and drew thousands to his side of the Jordan River. But he had defied Herod Antipas—the decadent son of Herod the Great.

With the help of the Romans, Herod the Great had ascended to the throne of Israel and Judea. He was not a Jew, but an Idumean, whose people had only recently adopted the Jewish religion. Yet the Romans could not distinguish one Jew from another, they believed he could be an acceptable leader. Of course, he was a Roman puppet who contributed vast sums to the Roman politicians, but to the Jews, he was an abomination. Like so many military men, the Roman leaders had no sensitivity to the feelings of the local populace. Selecting an Idumean to support as king was worse than selecting a Roman general.

Herod was a ruthless and brutal leader. He put to death without hesitation any threat in his years in power. Throughout his own family, he murdered any threat to his rule, brutally suppressed every rebellion and killed off most of his own family, including wives and sons. In fact, he had murdered so many of his family and court, that it was said, with wry Jewish humor, that it was safer to be a pig than a family member in the palace of Herod. On Herod's death, his heirs and various upper level Romans vied to rule Palestine. Eventually, the Romans selected Herod Antipas—a pallid image of his great father. Because they did not expect much of him, the Romans only gave him a fourth of his father's realm—the wild and ungoverned area of Galilee. Antipas in turn, ignored any responsibility except the collection of taxes from which he received a healthy share. Galilee was left to weeds.

After hours of baptizing, John turned to the still abundant line of penitents over to an assistant and wearily climbed up the river bank to sit under a grove of palm trees. He sat on his now much-celebrated camel's hair coat, and toweled himself down with a cloth. Exhausted, he leaned against the trunk of one palm tree and closed his eyes. Even in repose, he was an impressive figure with long, sinewy arms and legs, and taut body on which every muscle and tendon seemed to be stretched. Leaning against the tree, he seemed to twitch like a bolt of lightning.

"Master, might we speak with you?" Two men dressed in dusty robes and ragged sandals approached hesitantly. They spoke with a strong Galilean accent and were large, broad-shouldered men obviously used to doing a hard day's work.

Wearily, John opened his eyes. "Yes. What can I do?"

"Master, we are humble fishermen from Capernaum near Tiberias. We have come to seek out the new preacher, Jesus the Nazarite, and seek your permission to do so." The men stood awkwardly and shuffled their feet while only occasionally stealing looks at John as he sat in front of them.

"What do you want?"

"We are leaders of a small Zealot group of rebels who have been protecting the Jewish farmers and trading caravans in the Galilee. The Roman soldiers and other bandits have been attacking and looting. The Zealots had been harassing and generally making control difficult for the Romans. As a result the Galilee had been relatively free of any government or security Roman presence for several years.

"Your Jesus is a Galilean, of the line of David, and we seek his counsel." The two men knew that their identities were safe with John, who had recently denounced Herod Antipas for divorcing his wife, Marianne, and marrying his sister-in-law, a sin under Jewish law. He knew Herod Antipas was debating some course of action so that John's denunciation would not go unpunished. Political factions of Jews had joined the pro-Herod side and others joined the pro-John the Baptist side. Generally, the choice of side was based on political expediency and had little to do with who was right. The Sadducees were stuck in the middle and froze in fear of joining either side. The public in Jerusalem, Sepphoris and the other cities watched the maneuvering of the political titans and kept score anxiously. It probably meant that John was a walking dead man even as he sat there in Bethbara.

"What are your names and who will vouch for you?" John would not fall so easily into a trap set by Roman or Herodian provocateurs.

"I am Peter, often called Simon, and this is my brother, Andrew. We had been fishermen until the Roman tax made our trade unprofitable. We are known to Bar Abbas." Disclosing this identity to any Roman agent would mean death, but, again, John was a man to be trusted. Bar Abbas was a code name adopted by a leader of the Zealots—it meant simply "Son of the Father," but to those sophisticated in Jewish revolutionary circles, it meant a powerful leader. Its disclosure was like a password.

"I know none of these men, but will make inquiries. Stay with us for a few nights while I send out for evidence of your good faith."

The men retired to the area of tents scattered among the trees along the Jordan River and set down their packs. They leaned on their unrolled tent and dipped their hunks of pita into a grape leaf filled with hummus.

Word eventually had come from Jerusalem vouching for Peter and Andrew as men of good standing in the Zealots. The men were now summoned to John who was again seated in the shaded palm tree grove. Jesus was summoned to appear. As soon as he was seated in front of John, John stared deeply at him and began to speak. "I am aware of your identities and will permit you to speak to Jesus, but I must warn you, He is a man of great piety and seriousness. He will surpass me as a preacher and will draw many to him. I realize I have sealed by doom by meddling in the affairs of those who claim the power to rule our land and our people. I should have answered only the call of Our Lord to aid in the cleansing of souls and preparing for the kingdom of God. But the public abomination of our venial and corrupt rulers could not go without disclosure. I hope Jesus may resist the same temptation and remain an advocate for the kingdom of God."

"Jesus is not like me. He has been educated throughout the region and is a man of great learning and curiosity. He has lived with Essenes, with the learned men of Alexandria. He has studied the Greek culture and philosophy. He has discussed and debated and read with our neighbors from Babylon, yet He remains a man of little pretense. His devotion to the way of truth and salvation of man is unshakable.

"My days are numbered. I have become nothing more than a pawn in a political chess game and will be removed from the board shortly. But, please, let Jesus not become such an object. He can surpass me easily and should not become involved in temporal matters. He must prepare the way for the Messiah and not be deterred.

"I will encourage his departure to the land of Galilee and wish him well. Simon and Andrew, I place him in your care. These are dangerous times and I would expect you to preserve him and his message."

CHAPTER SEVEN

Jesus Leaves John with Peter and Andrew

WHEN JESUS HAD COME up from the path of the grove of trees, he met John and the two men.

"Jesus," John started. "Those two men have come from the Zealots to bring you to meet their associates. The Zealots are a band of brave men who resist the Romans and the abomination they spread over our land."

Jesus knew well who they were and what the Zealots did. They were an underground guerilla force who harassed the Romans at every opportunity and often attacked and killed Jews who had been seen as assisting the Roman occupation. Out of courtesy, he let John, his revered mentor, explain himself.

"I, as you well know, am doomed; my following is doomed and many of my followers may be doomed. I have spoken out against Antipas for his adulteries and murders, for the wickedness of his ways and the sacrilege he visits daily on our lands and our religion. He claims to be a Jew and has curried favor with the Romans who have put him over us. This pretender, not a Jew, but an Idumean, is a constant embarrassment to our laws and people..."

Jesus could tell that John was about to begin a full-blown sermon and attack on the evils of Antipas and the revenge of God on him. It was a subject to be avoided if any further business could be conducted. He gently interceded, and got John back to the issue.

"Ah, yes. In any case, my mission must be continued by you. I have chosen you as my successor, and entrust my followers to you. I know you will continue on faithfully in our tradition. I also know you will exceed me and accomplish great things.

"You have my blessing and my warning. I warn you to avoid the traps I have fallen into. I have allowed my mission to be compromised by making it part of the political world, the world of men. You must seek the kingdom of God. The Messiah will usher in this kingdom only when men are ready in their hearts to receive it. We must prepare for the coming of the Lord by opening men's hearts. I allowed myself to be distracted from my purpose and my calling by confronting Herod.

"These men wish to take you to the Galilee where you will be able to start your ministry and open men's hearts to the way of the Lord. Do not become involved in the politics. These Romans and their puppet leaders and collaborators are too strong in the material world. In the spiritual world, they have no power. You must avoid their intervention. If not, evil will befall you as it has me.

"While Antipas has jurisdiction in Galilee, he lives in Jerusalem and will not harm you. You can preach to the souls of men throughout Galilee where neither the Romans nor Herod can harm you. You are Galilean; you are a descendant of David and you are a man of God. You will do much good in Galilee.

"Follow these men. They and their associates will protect you and provide you sanctuary. Leave me and fulfill our mission."

By this time, Jesus was overcome. John had found in him the essence of what he had come to understand about man and God and saw the purpose of his mission. John had brought him from a passive scholar to a preacher to men, a man called by God to prepare the way for the kingdom of God. It was difficult to leave, yet he knew John spoke the truth; he was doomed by his contact with Antipas. The politics of man is a dirty and defiling business; it corrupts those who engage in it. The kingdom of man was not the kingdom of God. It was now his duty to prepare men for the kingdom of God. He embraced John and both wept for some time. At last, John took Jesus by the arms and said, "Go; you will exceed me; go."

Jesus turned and followed the two Zealots onto the road to the wilderness across the Jordan.

CHAPTER EIGHT

Jesus Goes to Nazareth

THE TRAIL THROUGH THE wilderness was not easy. The wilderness was indeed a strange world. In places, there were simply rolling gray hills of hardened mud and stones baked by the sun to a dull gray. Occasional thorny acacias showed through the surface. As they went further, larger and larger hills rose up out of the floor. The surfaces were perforated by crags and caves over the pitted face. As the two men led the way by no known signs, they began to ascend along a diagonal line across the face of an escarpment. There almost appeared to be worn footholds in the path that were covered with rubble and dust. As they approached the saddle between two large hills which by now towered over the floor below, they made a left directly over the saddle and came to a point where they could see for several miles in what appeared to be a northerly direction. From behind them over their right shoulders, a strange cackling birdcall came from the other side of the saddle. About ten minutes later, another cackling birdcall from their left. The cackling noises followed them for the next few hours. Shortly thereafter, a teenage boy sat on a boulder above the path. The two Zealots murmured some inaudible sounds and the boy murmured back. As they came around another bend, there was a small mouth to a cave. The two Zealots squatted down and crawled through the entrance, and motioned Jesus to follow.

As Jesus came through and felt for the walls on the sides of the cave, he still could not see. His eyes were still adjusting from the sun outside and he could feel or see nothing as he began to stand up slowly. Eventually, he could see a room about the size of a house carved out of the rock with doors leading out in each direction. A small fire burned in the middle of the room and some five men sat or leaned around the fire. A pot of lentils was bubbling slowly over the fire and several dishes of hummus were distributed around the hearth.

"Sit! Sit! You've come a long way. Sit! And eat! Eat! You must be hungry." The smaller of the men seated across from him spoke and slowly came into view. He was draping his fingers around a piece of bread into the hummus. Jesus sat. Actually, he was very thirsty from the long walk. As if on cue, a woman came through one of the openings with a goatskin of water. Jesus gulped at the water and ate the hummus for several minutes before looking up. Finally, he sat back against the wall and looked around the group.

"Do you know who we are?" The small man said.

"Of course, the Zealots. What do you want with me?"

"For now, just your time…to listen."

"Here I am." He spoke a familiar biblical response from the bible when men have been sought out by God. The men assembled chuckled in recognition of the biblical response of one called to fulfill a divine mission.

"We want to support your ministry as you preach through the Galilee. We can provide protection, places to stop, and welcome in towns throughout. That is all. We want you to preach as you have done with John."

"I am certainly interested. John sent me to the Galilee to do just that, but how can I help you? What will you ask me to do?"

"Nothing. You are a descendant of David and a learned master. You will bring our northern brethren hope and unity. Now, the Galilee is a divided series of towns and outlying farms. Bandits prey on the weak throughout. The Roman legions send out parties from time to time, but, when they have passed, the bandits return. Some of the bandits are our own people—dispossessed from their land by taxes; some just rabble from neighboring tribes looking for something to steal. Our people need to unite and communicate with one another and to have hope."

"How will you do this?"

"You will preach of the Messiah and the necessity of man to prepare for the Messiah."

"There is nothing so new in that. You have Pharisees who preach that message every day. Why me? And what do you want me to preach? I am different from the Pharisees in many ways. I have my own vision."

"We have heard your message and many of us have attended your sermons. We want you to continue your ministry as you wish. We are not religious scholars, we are of course Jewish but we do not wish to impose ourselves in religious matters. You have the power and calling we don't. Many of the Pharisees are small-minded, little men who are easily entangled in unnecessary complexities and ritual. You command attention. You will succeed where they have failed. We have resources throughout Galilee and can provide money, places to stay, safe passage and bodyguards. We only want you to do what you have done under John's aegis."

"We expect you to give the people hope and unify them in their desire for the coming of the Messiah. As you know, we Jews are a fractious lot. Given the opportunity, we will dispute anything and form factions. We can be distracted by other religions. The Sadducees have their followers, the Pharisees, theirs. There are Roman collaborators and assimilationist Jews who would be Greek or Roman. Not to mention those who have some connection to Judaism like Samaritans, Idumeans and other sects that have fallen away from mainstream Judaism. We need you to unite them and inspire them to the faith of our fathers."

Jesus listened and calmly ate the lentil broth. As the other elders of the Zealots began to speak, his mind drifted. "It is strange that I am eating this lentil stew at this crossroads in my life. Jacob took his birthright for Esau for a lentil stew. Cain slew Abel over a lentil stew. Imagine the fate of our people is dependent on lentil stew. But I have little choice. John, poor John is doomed. His ministry will die after he is dead. I must continue his ministry, and I may be under the watchful and vengeful eye of Antipas if I stay on the Jordan River. Galilee is safe for me. It is my home. People will welcome me, and these Zealots will protect and support me. I am of age. I must begin my ministry now."

As yet another speaker began to importune Jesus, he interrupted. "Enough. Enough. Yes, I am interested in your proposal and welcome it. When can we start and what will you do?"

"Peter, here, will be your bodyguard and treasurer when Judas is not with you. Your contact among us will be Judas. We will come to join your band of followers from time to time. You will not know our real names. You may call me Bar Abbas. Andrew will assist Peter and will answer to Judas. You may stay with us and learn our ways—our passwords, our signs and symbols. We will not involve you in our activities, but will keep you apprised through Peter and Andrew of our cause."

Jesus then was taken on a tour of the complex of caves making up the Zealot compound. The caves were ingeniously dug out of the dried mud, rock and limestone into the mountain. Throughout, there were minute borings for air. Where water had trickled in from catch areas on the mountainside, it ran into cisterns. In cooking areas, vents had been bored through the walls to let the heat and smoke escape. There were many vacant rooms carved along the low, narrow corridors. During the tour, Jesus passed men and women busy carrying out chores of one sort or another. Occasionally, he could see stockpiles of weapons, including many Roman uniforms, breastplates, shields and swords. There were about fifty men in the complex now, but it could easily accommodate at least two hundred fifty who could hide for days surviving on the food and water stored there.

"We have many more of the hideouts scattered both in the Judea and the Galilee. We can harass and strike at the Romans on patrol and then disappear from sight in a matter of minutes. Some of these hideouts date back to the days of the Assyrians and Babylonians. We have always been a difficult people to subjugate, and we have made every occupation an expensive one for our enemies. Since the days of Solomon, we have been subjects of one foreign ruler or another. We have become excellent guerilla warriors in the style of David."

"And yet, in these hideouts, we maintain a proper Jewish lifestyle. We have ritual baths, altars, and synagogues, and we store our torahs in proper arks with proper adornments. We store our scrolls and the Talmud in study rooms, and we educate our boys for their Bar Mitzvah."

"And yet, in no time, we can camouflage the exterior of these caves so that we cannot be discovered. We can seal up these caves, especially in the wilderness, so that they can rest in repose for centuries."

Jesus began to learn the code words and hand signs the Zealots used in communicating with one another. He would be taught to use them in his sermons to communicate with those who were not among his own followers, but other Zealots who came to observe his progress. The process took no time at all and soon Jesus was ready to venture out on his way with Peter and Andrew.

At daybreak, they left through a different cave entrance on the floor of the desert and started their trek north with a fully laden donkey.

"I must say, master, that it was Peter and I who told the Zealots of you. We have operated as part of the band in the area of Capernaum. Most of our band consists of fishermen or farmers so heavily taxed that they cannot feed their families. The Zealots recruited us and gave us hope and direction.

"John and you have become known as far north as the small towns around the sea of Galilee. Some of our Zealots returned from John, and could speak only of you for days. Peter and I have been to see you several times and want to learn from you and attend you as you preach."

Peter, Andrew and Jesus began the long walk to Nazareth. After some discussion, the three had decided to start Jesus' ministry in his hometown, where he would be known and recognized. Jesus had left the town nearly fifteen years before to begin his wanderings and search for meaning. Only vestiges of his Galilean accent remained and he had assumed the language of the educated men and foreign ideas he had acquired in his travels. John had instructed him to lower his tone and to address his sermons to the common man and not the Pharisean scholars, and over his time with John, he had begun to speak more plainly and communicate with the pilgrims to Bethbara more easily.

He learned to give examples from everyday life to make his point. These parables spoke directly to the Galileans.

As they walked over the gray rubble of the desert wilderness and into the green hills of upper Galilee, the three discussed all the changes and problems the Galileans faced. The overwhelming tax burden which chased men and their families from their farms, and the fishing boats at the Sea of Galilee. The men had resorted to forming bands of roving bandits who attacked the caravans and raided residential settlements. Everyone was suffering—not only the Jews, but the Samaritans and a variety of other ethnic groups. What was left of the northern kingdom was now inhabited by a polyglot of ethnic groups, all of whom shared in the fear and poverty in the region.

Many of those in Galilee were poor farmers or those recently dispossessed from their land. The taxes from the Romans and the tithes from the Sadducees were extremely onerous. The Romans exacted at least a quarter of the crop each year and the tithe was one eighth. There was a second tithe from the temple for the poor and a third tithe every third year as well as a tithe equal to one half of the produce from the land every seventh year. In addition there were other charges such as road tolls and custom duties levied. Frequently, the collection of these taxes were delegated to private agents who had purchased the right to collect these taxes and kept a portion of the collection. Frequently, they embezzled part of the collection, causing the Romans in turn to put a higher quota on the people. If the peasants had little left to feed their families, they often simply left their farms and joined bands of wandering brigands. Their hatred of the tax collectors known as publicans made them one of the most sought after targets for robbery and assassination. Usually, the entire family of the tax collector was ostracized from the community. Those residents who were not strict in paying their tithes to the temple were also ostracized and treated with contempt. In those times, the numbers of angry unemployed or overtaxed peasants were growing daily.

After Rome had assumed control of the area, it had been largely neglected. Theoretically, it was under the control of the Tetrarch of Syria, but the jurisdiction had been given to Herod Antipas, who had assumed the duties from his father when Jesus was about eight. In the ensuing years, Herod Antipas had remained, for the most part, in Judea, pleasuring himself at various palaces in Jerusalem, Masada or Caesarea—all in the area of the former southern kingdom well protected by the Roman legions. Antipas pursued primarily a life of indulgent pleasure supported by taxes from the region of Galilee and east. In return, he gave his constituents virtually nothing—no police protection, and little in the way of justice, commerce, or roads. His constituents hated him and he ignored them. Only the justice system and community structure of the Jews provided what little stability there was in the region. The people were desperate and miserable, and talk of a messiah had been building for years—since the Maccabees had lost power over seventy years before. And the people sought a messiah.

The "messiah" held many meanings for many people. In days past, the messiah had been discovered and anointed by the high priest to be spiritual leader of the people. However, there was no agreement among the people. The Sadducees, a hereditary priestly cult, controlled the temple in Jerusalem. Their high priests, fearful of the Romans, had abdicated their influence and permitted the Roman procurator to select the high priest and cooperated with the Romans to preserve a peace: the "Pax Romana." The Sadducees claimed to be the exclusive priests of the Jews and controlled the operation of the Temple in Jerusalem. Only at the Temple could an animal sacrifice be offered. They controlled this lucrative function as one of the required rituals of Judaism. The Pharisees, a scattered group of religious leaders, officiated and preached at synagogues throughout Palestine. They saw salvation in firm adherence to Jewish law and ritual as atonement for their sins. More often than not, their insistence on correct behavior was excessive and petty. In theory, once sins had been properly expiated through prayer and atonement, God would provide a messiah as He had in past Jewish history. It was unclear whether God would provide a military leader like David or a spiritual leader like Elijah or enlighten the foreign ruler to free the Jews as God had done with Ramses in Egypt, or Cyrus in Persia, or Ahasuerus for Esther.

Jesus, as he walked, was unsure as to who he was. Essentially, he sought only to be a humble preacher like John who would provide hope to the many miserable people of the Galilee. He certainly was not a military man and had no interest in the wealth and political trappings of a king. He entered the lawless region of Galilee with two bodyguards provided by the Zealots who promised to protect Him and provide for His followers. He hoped to pursue an itinerant ministry among the scattered towns. If he was successful, he would garner a reputation and be welcomed in the towns he came to.

Nazareth, the family home, appeared to be the safest and most welcoming place to start his new profession. On arriving, all of his family members would swell with pride, as he this new protégé of John preached to the congregation. On Saturday morning, he took his place among the congregants and awaited his time.

As usual and by practice since time immemorial, the Jewish Sabbath service began as Jesus and the two Zealots sat among the townspeople. First, as the congregants entered, they joined in chanting several psalms. Then, an elder of the community wrapped in his prayer shawl recited the Ten Commandments and then changed the "Shema"—"Hear, O Israel, the Lord Our God, the Lord is One." The elder then changed the Eighteen Benedictions, joined at various times by the congregation this age-old ritual. Then, the sacred scrolls of the Torah were removed from the wooden ark and read by some selected members of the village in Hebrew. Each week, the new portion was read, and each week, members of the community were chosen to read part of that week's portion.

Jesus' old hometown had prospered over the years. It was a short donkey ride to Sepphoris, the main city of the north where many trade routes crossed. After the Romans had destroyed it years earlier, it had rebuilt and was now wealthy. The old residents of Nazareth had prospered with it. They were no longer poor or meek, but conservative and contented.

On this Saturday, Jesus asked to be given a portion to be read and later explained in Aramaic—the vernacular at that time. Jesus had carefully selected the portion and began to read an important passage from Isaiah:

"The spirit of the Lord God is upon me, because the Lord hath anointed me to preach good tidings unto the meek; He hath sent me to bind up the broken hearted, to proclaim liberty to the captives, to proclaim the acceptable year of the Lord and the day of vengeance of our God…" (Isa 62: 1-2.)

A murmur spread throughout the congregation. "Who is this? What arrogance! He the anointed—how dare he claim that chapter—who is he? Wait, wait, I know he is the son of Mary and the brother of James…and Joses and Judas… and Simon… Yes, we know him—he is Joseph's son. He is Mary's son come back to Nazareth to tell us he is anointed by God."

The congregation began to turn to Mary in the women's section where she sat with her daughters. Mary and the girls shrank back from the latticework on the second floor women's section.

Jesus then stood and faced the men and said, "This day is the scripture fulfilled in your ears."

The murmuring grew louder. "Who is he, again? What arrogance—he the anointed, he the messiah…he claims the Spirit of the Lord… he says we are the meek, the broken hearted…he dares preach to us." The crowd pressed around him, and he, Simon and Andrew, arose and walked down the aisle. Simon and Andrew drew closer to Jesus as some of the men began to shove them and yell at them. Jesus moved faster until he was outside on the slope leading to the front door.

"You may say to me, 'physician heal yourself,' but I say… 'A prophet is without honor in his own land.'"

This taunt to the now angry crowd stoked their ire even more.

The murmurs and shouts followed. "Now he is a prophet we should honor…Where does he get the courage to say these things? What an insult! A prophet now he is! Mary's little boy wants us to glorify him!"

Jesus now stood on a bench and addressed the crowd. "I will tell you a story: There were many widows in Israel in the days of Elizah, but there had been a drought for three and one-half years and everyone was suffering from a famine, but the Lord sent no aid to those widows. Instead, the Lord sent Elizah to a widow in Sarepta, a Canaanite, not even a Jew and He comforted her. And another time, the prophet Elisha was sent not to the lepers in Israel of which there were many, but he saved Naaman, the Syrian."

51

By this time, the crowd was seething. "Now our own God won't save us, but he saves the gentiles. When did the gentiles pay their share! Our boy Jesus, all of a sudden he's Elizah and Elisha and he's helping the infidels. Who does he think he is? We have it bad enough and we have to listen to this…Does he think we are stupid? …He comes back after all this time and thinks we should make him a prophet."

With that, Jesus, Simon and Andrew were in full retreat and ran toward the village with the crowd in hot pursuit. As they reached the gorge, some of the younger men grabbed Jesus by his cloak and only when Simon drew his sword did they let him go. All three took off for the hills.

As they lay among the rocky crags on a hill several miles from town, Jesus and the others panted and lay groaning on their backs unable to move. Jesus sat staring at his sandals. "Well that doesn't seem to be the best approach." As they eventually recovered, Peter was still mad and began to rail against the ignorance of the townspeople.

Andrew slowly rubbed his jaw where he had been struck by one of the young men. "Well, I think we'll have to save that town for later… Let's try the fishermen of Capernaum. We know them."

Jesus stared into the middle distance as he lay against a hillock of hardened gray hillside. This was the first of many times Peter and Andrew would see Jesus in this state. He had fallen into a deep reverie and stayed without moving for some time while Peter and Andrew paced about nervously.

"What am I doing here? I am an embarrassment now to my mother and family. I cannot do what John has done. The crowds do not respond to me. Should I go back to carpentry and raise a family? Should I become a teacher, a malamed, to the young boys?" His mood did not lighten. His chosen career path had a large roadblock in it and he for the first time was facing disaster. These people did not listen, they did not trust him. He had failed. Eventually, he rose and followed Peter and Andrew north to Galilee. He could only hope for better success in Capernaum.

CHAPTER NINE

Joseph at Caesarea

JOSEPH DISMOUNTED FROM HIS carriage. His entourage made a wonderful display. As he descended, his robes lined in silk fluttered in the wind. He was followed by several retainers as he was announced at the gates to the Procurator's residence at Caesarea.

The residence was a huge complex constructed by Herod the Great to please and appease the Romans to solidify him in his position as King of the Jews. The very existence of this palatial estate was viewed as an abomination to the Jews. Naming it after a human being was akin to raising that human to divine status, and constituted a graven image forbidden by the Ten Commandments. Even more so, it represented a currying of favor with the Romans and an excessive and obvious sop to the already swollen egos of the Roman leaders. More importantly, Herod was not an ethnic Jew, but an Idumean. His people had only recently converted and were not schooled as the rest of the Jews in the Torah. He had been picked by the Romans to serve as the titular ruler of the Jews, but subordinate to Roman rule. He was an outsider and trusted by no one; and therefore an easy figure for the Romans to use to control the Jews.

The complex for the Procurator consisted of an indoor and outdoor fresh water pool at the ocean giving the bathers a spectacular view of the Mediterranean. The palace adjoining it was huge and sumptuous, adorned with glittering mosaics whose tesserae occasionally sparkled with gold flecks. There were large flowing drapes of many colors with purple—the expensive Phoenician purple—predominating since it was a color reserved for emperors and royals. The deep blue dye derived from the clams of the Mediterranean also hung in large drapes. These were the colors of opulence. There were columns supporting the roof and the high ceilings which were strategically perforated with sky lights to allow the smoke and incense to rise and the sunlight and moonlight to illuminate the interior. It was a truly magnificent and inspiring throne room.

Pontius Pilate and Joseph of Harama Theo only ever met in this small antechamber. Many Jews considered it a sin for Jews to break bread with those who did not observe their strict dietary laws. Joseph was certainly interested in keeping his public image as acceptable to the general public as possible, but he was the more circumspect because he feared the sicarii. The sicarri were men known for carrying a small, but lethal, dagger and well known for using it to gut those Jews they considered to be collaborating with the Romans. When possible, they also attacked particularly difficult Roman officials who may have strayed from the safety of the Roman legions.

Joseph in Jewish public life had many images. As the heir of a line of well respected and very wealthy traders, he had interests in buying and selling goods of all sorts. His family had several cargo ships which traveled from Palestine to North Africa, Cyprus, Rome and even as far as Iberia. Some said he brought in tin from Britannia. The risks of piracy, weather and theft were extremely high, but the rewards were commensurate with the risk. Their boats were among the best; their crews were loyal, well paid and had been in the family service for years. Joseph also bought up farmland as the farmers defaulted on their loans or taxes. It was considered a crime in some quarters to take over these homesteads for defaulted taxes. If it were known that he had acquired the land, he would not be popular, and probably hated. However, Joseph's agent was known for granting favorable terms to the dispossessed farmers to remain on their farms as tenant farms. Once freed of the debts of Roman taxes, and given a percentage of the crop so that they could keep their family above subsistence level, the farmers could remain among his neighbors and survive. On the other hand, Joseph could control large amounts of the crop and, as a result, bargain more favorably on the prices. His political influence and occasional bribe could reduce the taxes. Of the absentee landlords, Joseph did not suffer the anger and hatred most felt.

And yet, for Joseph to be seen with Pilate at business dealings, his esteem rose tremendously. To have the ear of the Roman governor was a connection that many sought, but few attained. With Pilate having great power—subject only to minimal restrictions under Roman law, his decisions could be brutal and devastating or beneficial as he determined.

Immediately north and set back from the sea was an immense hippodrome. There was a series of banked rows facing the sea to overlook the large race track which could accommodate races of all sorts, but mainly humans and chariots. The floor of the hippodrome had several trap doors to allow animals or gladiators to enter as well as from the level gates at the sides. Gladiators would stage large mock battles against a backdrop of the Mediterranean for the spectator's delight.

But this week, the schedule called for the use of the amphitheater lying past and inland from the pools. When scheduled, the day of the amphitheater would include many events of both high and low entertainment. Because of its distance from the neighboring villages and cities, those who attended the events at either the amphitheater or the hippodrome were limited to the upper crust of Palestinian society and included Romans and Jews, as well as Greeks and the many other foreign nationals engaged in trade at the ports.

It was curious that Herod had erected this magnificent city and port in the southern end of the Galilee and intended it as the home base for the Roman legions when the Roman Procurator and the legions' jurisdiction was in the southern Kingdom of Judea, while Herod's palace was in Jerusalem, not in his jurisdiction of Galilee.

When Herod the Great first ruled this area for the Romans, his reputation for brutality and swift reprisals for crimes committed by the roving bands of brigands had pacified most of Galilee. There however was a continual re-supply of brigands from the poor and dispossessed. Family homesteads often were forfeited for non payment of taxes. Herod's superb military forces were quick to track and slaughter the miscreants. Herod Antipas was no match for his father. He had survived a brutal family bloodbath to become the Romans' designated overseer of this area. The Romans were certainly able to recognize the flaws of Antipas and put its own governor, now Pontius Pilate, over him, but still left him in charge of the Galilee. Antipas was more interested in indulging in fleshly pleasures and ignored the area, which now fell into virtual anarchy.

The Romans had the best of the situation. They collected the taxes and tribute from the wealthy and pacified southern province, but resided in the magnificent coastal city of Caesarea in southern Galilee. As Joseph strode with his retainers to the main gate of the palatial residence, he felt at ease. He was a wealthy descendant of a long line of traders and businessmen. His wealth gave him easy access to the existing rulers who were eager to have his educated, intelligent company as well as his local knowledge. He spoke many of the languages necessary for conducting business throughout North Africa, and the Roman Empire. He could converse with particular style and flair in Greek—the language of the educated and artist elite. He was respected and befriended as a man of wealth and culture, but he was particularly well connected to those in power because he never forgot to keep them well supplied with precious gifts befitting their station.

He moved equally well within Jewish society and was a respected member of the Sanhedrin, although neither a Sadducee or Pharisee.

But to a few, he was known as "ha Rama Theo"—an odd combination of Hebrew and Greek meaning "of the Highest of God." This appellation was corrupted to Arimathea to conceal its clandestine meaning, and represented to be a small town in the area which, in fact, did not exist. Joseph never explained his name and rather enjoyed the confusion and misdirection it caused. Its actual meaning and the group who had bestowed it upon him would remain a secret. Anyone with a last name had considerable prestige.

As a result, to Pilate, he was Joseph of Arimathea and greeted warmly as a favored guest. He was immediately taken to a small drawing room where the two shared political gossip and excellent wine, and platters of fresh fruit and cold seafood delicacies. Much aware of the Jewish dietetic restrictions, the local cooks served the fish and met all aspects of the strict code in the Torah. Although it was forbidden to dine with the non-Jews, it was a minor legal point that Joseph transgressed by accepting small hors d'oeuvres with his wine. And, very important politically. Joseph, through years of careful upbringing and breeding, was well aware of the practical necessities of ritual observation, while dealing with non-Jews.

After many of the latest topics were covered, Joseph reached inside the waist band and brought out a small kidskin bag. Opening the drawstring, he carefully let three small rubies dance on the marble table top.

"I recently got this shipment in and thought of you and your wife. Please see if she might be able to have them mounted in her tiara."

Pilate was an attractive, stylish man with a plump almost feminine face who had come from the equine classes in Rome, a seat of junior nobility. Although educated in the basics, he could never pretend to the gentlemanly body of knowledge Joseph had. Although professing knowledge of Greek, it was crude and his mind could not absorb the nuances and delicacy that language permitted an educated man to enjoy. His wife, however, was different. She came from Roman aristocracy. She was quite plump and had unruly coarse black curls which she rigorously tried to have twisted and pulled into the latest fashion. But she betrayed her inner nature with a perpetual pout and whine which suggested that she had been denied many things in life. Her marriage to Pilate had made his career from a lower level through several posts until this one in Palestine. He owed her much and was careful to appease her to avoid the wrath of her father and worse yet her mother. The rubies showed him to be a powerful and skilled provider to his constantly whining wife. It was this sort of cleverness that Joseph had acquired. To avoid the appearance of a bribe or *quid pro quo*, while both appealing to Pilate's need to appease and spoil his wife, this gift ingratiated Joseph in many ways. While not a direct bribe, Joseph knew it would be returned many times over.

Having covered all topics of mutual concern, Pilate rose to greet his many other guests for the day's entertainment at the amphitheater and Joseph left by the side door to draw as little attention to himself as possible.

The program for the amphitheater that day consisted of a variety of theatrical performances—from low farce with many crude and blasphemous skits to high Greek drama. The music also ran from crude and rowdy folk songs to refined poetry of the day.

The program began in mid-morning and lasted all day. Foods, including delicacies of all sorts, were served by vendors and they were the latest rage in Rome—door mice and baby quail on a skewer which had been roasted over a rotisserie after they had been marinated in olive oil and local spices.

The audience was securely segregated into certain sections by ethnicity. The Roman nobility adjoined Pilate and his wife in the main section over the arched entrance for the performers at the center. High ranking Roman officers were adjacent to the right of the emperor. To the right of them were foreign dignitaries, and merchants in good standing with the Procurator. To the left were the wealthier residents of Sepphoris who had made the trek to participate in the spectacle. As Roman subjects, they were given the least status and the lowest rank on the left of the Procurator. It was necessary to attend these assemblages from time to time since it displayed in public each family's rank in the social hierarchy. The wives insisted on attending in the best robes and all the gems her husband had acquired for her. Their eyes were lined with kohl and their hair oiled and fashioned with ribbons in the styles of the day. It was a major social event. The other levels ranged downward on the social scale to those barely able to afford the admission.

Since the proceedings included a variety of programs and lasted the entire day, all the groups of people often mingled with each other and did not adhere to the strict class lines their seating had dictated. As a result, it was an extraordinary opportunity to meet and make connections socially, and frequently in matters of business and politics. The wealthy Jews did not lose the chance to meet many Roman bureaucrats and officials whose acquaintance could be of an immeasurable advantage without actually sharing a meal with them. The bureaucrats were often salaried, and educated members of the

Roman middle class who envied the wealth and status of the Roman nobility. A chance to make money on the side was a way to add to their nest eggs and provide for the time when their political lives might not be so fortunate.

Communication between the Romans and Jews was difficult. Aside from the difference in wealth, the Romans were a crude and brutal lot with poor manners and little breeding. They ate gluttonously and spilled food and wine with great abandon. They rarely bathed and gave off a strong odor. They worshipped gods famous for their gross and barbaric behavior—rape, incest, murder, trickery were common themes of their gods. The Jews had strict dietary rules, were required to bathe and wear clean garments. They ate and spoke fastidiously and were often nauseated by watching the Roman enjoy the forbidden delicacies passed by the vendors. The wealthier Jews were educated not only in Jewish law, but in Greek literature and philosophy.

The Roman's customs provided that when they had enough wine and food, they would retire to the vomitorium, placed two fingers down their throats and regurgitated all they had eaten or drunk the previous few hours. Servants attended them while they did so by holding their robes and handing them scented face towels afterward. The Romans would then return to the feast and enjoy more of the delicacies and wine as before.

As Joseph moved down the row to his seat in the amphitheater, he froze. Passing him on the stone steps leading to the more elevated seats was Judas, known to a restricted few by his nom de guerre— the feared Judas Iscariot. Iscariot was not his family name; it was an epithet by which he was called by those who knew him only by rumor. He was a member of the dreaded sicarii—an underground secret group of Jewish rebels who carried small daggers, also called sicari, with extremely sharp points which could easily be concealed on their bodies—taped to their thighs or their buttocks. Their mission was to kill Jews who collaborated with the Roman occupation or attack Romans who strayed too far from the protection of their legions. Judas was taking a seat among the Jews currying favor with the Romans. It meant trouble. After all, there were Jews attempting to actually assimilate themselves into Roman culture by attending a Roman spectacle replete with crude satires which were often antisemitic, but certainly vulgar, with drama depicting Roman values and gods which often directly conflicted with Jewish beliefs and laws. In many ways, a Jew attending one of these functions was opting out of his heritage to join the Roman or actually Greek culture which reverent Jews considered in many ways an abomination. To set Judas in the cheaper seats to observe those Jews among the Romans was to put a fox in the chicken coop.

Many of the younger Jewish men had begun to affect the Greek and Roman ways. Of course, those cultures espoused the gymnasium—an activity where young men participated nude in athletic pursuits under the watchful eye of the older Romans, who enjoyed an occasional homo-erotic adventure. Wrestling, boxing, track and field events, archery and other Olympic style games were among the pursuits which took up several hours often daily of the leisure time of young Romans. Young Jews wishing to be accepted among this group could hardly appear naked without displaying the fact that they were circumcised. To assimilate properly, a young Jewish male would have to have a skin flap surgically re-attached to the end of his penis. There were cheaper versions which were simply elastic attachments of animal skin which could be rolled down over the end of the penis. The reattachment of the foreskin was an abomination. It was a denial of Abraham's covenant with God.

In another popular activity, the Greek and Roman males considered it a matter of high culture to engage in homosexual activity or mixed sexual activity involving young males in the baths, or prostitutes and several males. A Jewish male could hardly join in these without exposing to all his centuries-old heritage commencing with Abraham.

As Judas passed and caught Joseph's eye, he nodded ominously. Here were two men, known by reputation throughout the Jewish world, but whose identity was a closely guarded secret by the elite few. One was an underground assassin, the other a wealthy and connected merchant. But neither feared the other. Judas and his band were well aware of Joseph's contacts with the Romans, and very much appreciated the intelligence Joseph could frequently pass on concerning all aspects of the Roman occupation: when ships came and went, when and where Roman soldiers were displayed, who the Romans would arrest, and which officials could be bribed, blackmailed or otherwise neutralized. Joseph often provided money, safe houses, donkeys, clothing and hideouts to the different Jewish rebel groups. As a member of the Sanhedrin, Joseph could often leak out the directions or news of the deliberations. There was no mistaking Joseph's motives in attending this showy Roman spectacle; there was no mistaking where his loyalty lay. At the same time, there was no mistaking why Judas, in the garb of a wealthy and assimilated Jewish merchant, was in Caesarea sitting among the wealthy Jews in their assigned section of the amphitheater. Joseph shivered slightly as Judas passed.

It was now the mid-morning as the entertainment's agenda began to unfold. The producers had cleverly alternated high-minded drama with crude slapstick satires, devotional hymns and poems with high spirited dances by nearly naked slave women captured in Asia minor and to the easy, amazing feats of agility and strength from African men, and stirring erotic tableaux of naked women engaged in a variety of sexual positions.

As the sun had passed mid day and the afternoon grew even hotter making the vast quantities of wine the audience had consumed fermented in their brains, the people began to get rowdier and noisier, cruder and more boisterous, often interrupting and heckling the acts. Until a loud scream pierced the air as one of the guards ran to the stage and shouted at the Procurator and his assemblage of Roman soldiers, "He's dead. Oh, it's horrible. He's dead."

After the guards ran up to the man and calmed him down, he finally led them to the vomitorium. Somehow, the whole amphitheater became quiet as everyone strained to hear the man's story. Apparently, he had walked into the vomitorium which was strangely deserted and quiet. As he approached the vomiting tubs, he saw a pair of feet in the air with the body facing down into the stew of partially digested matter in the largest tub. The body was naked on the lower half with his robe pulled up over his head. The penis of the body had been severed and was inserted in his rectum with the un-circumcised head pointing upward. Blood flowed over the marble tub and floor of the room. The head was not visible, but was resting up to the shoulders in about ten inches of vomit. There were several puncture marks from a small, but sharp, instrument which also had pierced the rectal area and caused small rivulets to dribble down the sides of the marble tub. There was chaos in and around the vomitorium from the audience who pushed and elbowed for an opportunity to view the gruesome scene.

As the guards pulled the body out and threw water on the face, the features became clear. It was Simon, son of Eliahu, a wealthy Sepphoris resident. Among his occupations were the collection of taxes in an area, and the ownership of lands from those farms sold to pay taxes. Simon was in his late teens and was attending a Greek school along with other Romans. He was a plump and indulgent boy who enjoyed all the pastimes with the Roman youth. The cause of his death was obvious, the motive for his death was equally as obvious. Eliahu would be notified immediately.

The Roman general, eventually took charge of the scene and had the soldiers clear a large perimeter around the vomitorium. "Where are the attendants? Who are they? Bring them here immediately." Immediately, fifteen or twenty soldiers spread out in different directions and fifteen more sealed off all egress from the amphitheater area.

Of course, Judas was not found, but the attendants of the vomitorium were found bound and gagged behind several large bushes in the rear of the building. Otherwise, they were unharmed. They could not describe their attackers, but noted that they were swarthy and spoke Aramaic. They wore dark cloths over their faces. There seemed to be three of them, but possibly more.

News of the attack spread quickly and became exaggerated over time. It was clear that some underground Jewish group, probably the sicarii, had attacked the pampered son of a Jew who was collaborating with the Romans directly under the nose of the Procurator in his own well-guarded city of Caesarea. It sent shivers down the spine of the Roman elite and their Jewish collaborators.

CHAPTER TEN

Pilate—Introduction

A S THE TWO GENERALS conferred with Pilate, he was dwarfed by them. Pilate was a small, attractive man. Like most Roman citizens, he had a long aquiline nose and a plump, almost feminine, face. His hair was fashionably arranged in curls. His toga had an edging of the very expensive stitching in purple and gold thread. As he sat on the sella—a throne-like chair—in the secretarium—an enclosed room for secure meetings or trials—talking to the generals, he was very much aware of his position. He had astutely married a very well-born but distant member of Augustus' family, which had obtained for him a number of bureaucratic postings over the years. But the assignment as governor of Palestine was the crowning achievement of his career to this point.

The position of governor had essentially two functions: keep the peace over the conquered land and collect an abundant amount of taxes to be shipped to Rome. The peace or Pax Romana, as it was called, meant that, throughout the empire, a very specific policy would be followed. The conquered peoples were to be allowed to follow their own religious practices and, where appropriate, follow their own local customs, have their own leaders, and administer their own laws. In short, if they kept the peace and paid their taxes, they would not suffer much interference from the Romans in their daily lives, and could govern themselves.

On the other hand, if they continued to rebel and undermine Roman authority and law, they would suffer overwhelming and brutal consequences. Vast numbers of the opposition would be slaughtered in confrontations and the leaders would be exposed to the most painful and public torture and death possible—the crucifixion. The body of the leader would be posted onto a tau cross with his arms tied to the arms of the tau. Thus suspended, the leader, formerly a figure of veneration, would die slowly and painfully for several days while he slowly suffocated with the weight of his body pressing down on his lungs. Often, he wailed pitifully in his sufferings over the two or three days it took for him to die. The display was enough to shrivel the courage of any of his followers who might wish to succeed him as leader of the rebellion.

In the cruelest manner, as the leader would faint from the pain, the Roman guards would jostle him awake or shove cloths saturated with vinegar under their noses to revive them. Anyone below what was considered a leader was sold into slavery. There was a very profitable business in the sale of slaves. Even now, the Roman peninsula was beginning to suffer from the influx of slaves because this cheap labor forced the Roman citizens out of jobs. Slaves sold in the large cities of the conquered nations drew large bids at the auctions. Often, they had valuable skills in reading and writing, speaking several languages or making implements in iron, copper or brass, or as refined house servants. The peasants from the countryside would only go for heavy manual labor. More frequently, the more attractive females and young boys satisfied the increasingly more demanding and creative desires of the Romans with enough money to procure them. Others were sold to whoremongers who grew rich on the trade the slaves' bodies attracted.

Having achieved the rank of Procurator, Pilate now had the opportunity to amass a large amount of wealth. As the taxes were assessed and collected, it was taken for granted that, as part of his office, he would keep sums for himself and close members of his ruling authority as long as Rome's share was deemed adequate by Rome. As long as he met or exceeded, by small percentages, his predecessor's shipments to Rome, he could keep the rest and spread some among his loyal entourage.

On the other hand, if Palestine proved too rebellious and difficult to govern, he could, with a simple command to his legions, sack the treasury of the people, invade the rich houses and loot the country of its wealth and sell its people into slavery. The current policy of Rome, however, was to keep the peace and bleed the country slowly of its taxes. Although, Pilate was always conscious of the quick profit to be made by looting the country and selling off its residents. Under those circumstances, however, the Roman legions would get the lion's share of the looting and Pilate would be recalled to some as a failure.

He was also conscious of the military. Pilate was a civilian and a politician. His strength came from the powerful people his wife's family knew. They were the rich and powerful among the nobility and merchants. But the military was another force. He was well aware of the mistrust the military felt of the politicians and the jealousy they felt for his wealth and position. The soldiers looked with disdain at the politicians and bureaucrats who enjoyed the riches and spoils the soldiers procured for them. It is true that he had served an obligatory term in the army as a staff attaché, but he was never at the actual infantry level. The military was a hard life. Men could be separated from their families for five years or more and live in difficult conditions in foreign lands. They could march for miles with little food and water. Yet, it was an opportunity to move up in the world. After many years of faithful service, they could retire on a small farm and lead a life of ease. If they were fortunate to catch the eye of a centurion or someone of high rank, they could move up into a command position. But the real benefit of being a soldier was in the opportunity to sack, loot and rape. In the confusion of battle, in the aftermath of conquest, the ability to go into the homes of the rich and take their goods, to eat their precious delicacies and drink their fine wines and to have absolute unfettered mastery over their women were the priceless moments of heady excess. The right to pillage and ravage was inherent in the occupation of every soldier to pay for the days, months and years of privation. It was often the sole motivation for the common soldier to join the military. And the three legions of Roman soldiers assigned to Judah looked greedily at the fine houses and fancy women of Jerusalem, Sepharis, Caesarea, Jaffa and the other many fine cities throughout Palestine. Meanwhile, they lounged in the comfortable barracks in Caeserea and Jerusalem and except for daily drills and combat training waiting for the day they would be needed. Their superior armament and military tactics could cut through the ranks of mere peasant opposition like a knife through warm goat cheese. They would be absolute masters of the world when the time came, and they were eager for war.

The generals eyed Pilate with scorn. His puny arms and soft hands, his perfumed hair and fine toga was a foppery they ridiculed at the barracks. These men had been through years of weapons training. They could fight any man from anywhere in the world with any weapon and bring him low. They were an unparalleled fighting force that could defeat anyone in the world and had—from the Gauls, the Persians, the Thracians, the Spaniards. Weeks and months spent marching through rain, mud, snow, over mountains, through swamps, had made them hard mentally and physically. Even in the peace of Caeserea, they trained daily with their men, and engaged in athletic, military, simulated contests. At that time, no other military group could dare stand up to them. Many of them belonged to the Mithra religion which further fortified them by secret rituals and practices which were unknown to the upper classes. And yet, they had to take orders from this puny popinjay who spoke in the fancy accents of his Roman precinct. At this time, the politicians controlled the military, but the military organization was always strong and unified, ready to follow their generals in a coup to seize political power. The generals regularly communicated with their superiors in Rome and reviewed Pilate's activities in detail. One bad word from them and the military could exert a powerful and undeniable influence on the politicians and Pilate's golden career opportunity was over.

Pilate had not gotten to his position by accident. Years of politics had taught him the ability to manipulate and control the use of power and the appearance of the control of power. He assiduously involved the generals in his decisions and shared some of his tax collections with them. He was happy to receive their advice on military matters especially where crowd control and intimidation of the native population were involved. Where the concentration of resistance were situated, what groups among the conquered peoples caused the most trouble and what ones were most unhappy with the occupation. Their warnings of any impending problems were not to be ignored. Their advice was a valuable tool in controlling this conquered land. They maintained a well paid spy force to penetrate and identify rebel groups or uprisings.

"This holiday is a dangerous time, your excellency. Jerusalem normally has a population of 25,000. With this holiday, there are more than 250,000 pilgrims. Normally, we have shopkeepers, and temple workers. Now, we don't know who has come to town," Gallious said. He was a senior general and had served throughout the empire. He wore the toga of the army but still looked like he had his leather breastplate underneath. His massive arms were crossed over his chest as he leaned back in his seat in front of the governor. His face looked like an abused dog with scars across his brow and a long puncture in his cheek. There was no mistaking the crude native intelligence in his manner. He spoke with authority and was used to being in command. His manner, now alone with Pilate, displayed that he considered him an equal. In front of the public he, as required, deferred to Pilate and showed him great respect. "This provocation could create a lot of mischief." He did not seem concerned that a bunch of religious fanatics could put a dent in the tenth legion stationed in Jerusalem for the Passover. The army had already imposed a curfew after 9:00 P.M. on the streets of Jerusalem. They already inspected the baggage of all parties entering the walls of Jerusalem. An open massed conflict against the might of the tenth legion—and its men—assembled in Jerusalem was not an unreasonable consideration. "Yes, mischief, I would say. No more. But, of course, mischief can encourage more serious action."

CHAPTER ELEVEN

Jesus—early visit to Bethany

Early Ministry

JESUS AND THE DISCIPLES tramped slowly along the dusty path to Bethany. There were about fifteen men of various ages and sizes. Often, a group of women including occasionally the wives of the disciples rode in carts behind them. As was often the case, Judas and Simon had returned to other duties for the Zealots and the Sicarii. From the way they left, something was brewing and they were needed. In their place, a few younger Zealots had joined Peter, Andrew and the others as bodyguards for the Master as he was now known.

In the few months as he had wandered the upper Galilee, Jesus had begun to change. When Peter and Andrew first came to John the Baptist's site on the Jordan, Jesus had been a shy, intense, scholarly preacher whose innate religious fervor had attracted pilgrims to him almost in spite of himself. He lit up only when speaking to a group. Then he ignited with a fervor that overwhelmed and inspired the crowd. Some natural inbred fire was undeniably part of his demeanor and the ordinary men picked up on it immediately. He was drawing on an inspiration and an internal fire that must be believed.

His sermons had initially been scholarly, philosophical inquiries into religion and morals. Because they came from his own personal thoughts, they occasionally transgressed traditional Pharisaic or Sadducaic principles and even Jewish law itself. He could not help referring at times to the many religions or philosophies he had studied in the years since he left his mother and other siblings to wander the known world in search of enlightenment. By the time he left Nazareth, he had been well-schooled by the Pharisees and had exhausted the abilities of the local Pharisaic rabbinate. He had been sent with his family's blessing to study in Jerusalem with the independent Jewish sages who congregated around the Temple and held open-air discussions much in the manner of the Greeks. There he had learned to be sensitive to the political factions and movements that were boiling up against the so called Pax Romana that had come to control his country and fellow Jews.

Occasionally, he would visit his family and, on the way, stop at Sephoris or Caesarea to study with the Greek and Roman scholars who held open-air seminars and discussed Plato and the other pagan philosophers. This taste of forbidden fruit had proved alluring and drew him beyond the dictates of Jewish law and ritualism. After this irresistible temptation drew him to seek out the Zoroastrians to the east where he was welcomed in the remaining Jewish community in Babylon. Eventually he had heard of the large Jewish community in Alexandria and he had wandered down to Egypt. There he studied the variances between the Egyptian Judaism and the homegrown version in Jerusalem. He also was drawn to the wisdom of the Egyptian scholars whose lore went back of 2,500 years. In spite of their worship of idols and their deifying of the rulers, their religion had opened his mind to new and subtle religious themes.

In short, he studied and absorbed the essence of many of the current religions. He was seeking to distill some basic elements that must be part of a basic belief and a basic way that would lead to the coming of the Messiah and bring God's kingdom to this world. Somehow, someway, he felt the answer lay in the relationship of man and religion. He was relentless in his pursuit and questioning of each religion's most scholarly advocates to find some key, some combination which would would lead.

Of course, as a Jew, he constantly returned to Judaism for comparison and answers. Yet, each time he found a kernel of wisdom from some obscure text or scholar, he could not help but incorporate it in his own teachings. Of course, he had early on rejected the cyclical teachings of the nature religions. They viewed nature, the cycle of the seasons, the sun, the moon and the birth and death of life as a manifestation of what must be God. As a result, they worshipped fertility, and looked to the astrological changes as guides to their lives. It made man like an animal and permitted him to engage in animal acts like cruelty, murder and theft without punishment. The gods also behaved like animals and engaged in murder, trickery, incest and other practices, subjugating weaker people in turn. The stronger could conquer and dominate the weaker, plunder their gods, rape their women and force them into slavery. That could not be God's way. Judaism had placed responsibility on man to progress beyond bestial practices and raise him above the animals and practice morality. Man was to be the steward of animals and have dominion over them. It provided guide posts with many well-reasoned laws designed to govern human communities in a logical man-made way. The Jews had, for many years, been debating and analyzing passages from the Torah to create a steadily progressive approach to the ideal world where peace could prevail. It was difficult to find elements in these other religions which improved on the idea that man was above the animals and must govern himself.

The Greeks, alone, were the strongest influence Jesus had found to combine with Jewish principles. The Greeks spoke of actions which were inherently good or bad, and correct behavior could be determined by logical thinking and intuition. The moral force of Plato and Socrates placed with man the individual responsible for his own acts and required man to intuit correct actions for himself. This, of course, differed from Judaism which relied on the development of the law to help man a well-governed society and priests to interpret it for them. Jesus began to feel that man could discover the truth for himself and govern himself by his own internal moral force if properly enlightened; however, he could not ignore that many, without some external guide such as the law, might often persuade themselves that some improper temptation they could not resist might be the proper action. Man was thus in conflict between the rigidity of laws and the variability of man's appetites: the spiritual and the physical. Although he was raised as a Pharisee and felt an allegiance to the Pharisaic tradition, he often ran afoul of their overly strict adherence to rituals and practices, but very much supported their strict adherence to basic Jewish principles.

Now, as the dusty band of Jesus and disciples trundled into Joseph's farm in Bethany, they were tired and hungry. Joseph of Bethany was known by many names, including one given to him by some organizations to which he belonged. Joseph was also known as Arimathea. He was one of numerous wealthy people who contributed to Jesus' ministry and provided them food and shelter on the journeys. Many wealthy men and women joined the band of disciples as they would go from one small Galilean city to another.

As Jesus came to the door, two women greeted Jesus. One was Martha—the daughter of Joseph and the other was Mary, originally from the small town of Magdala, and Martha's cousin. Mary had been enamored of Jesus since she was in her early teens and met Jesus on one of his trips home from his wanderings. Many times, it had been suggested that Mary be betrothed to men of the better families in Galilee, but had managed to convince her family not to have her marry. Now, at the age of twenty-six, she was an anomaly among Jewish women, who usually married by an arranged marriage in their early teens. But, Mary came from a wealthy family and had been educated not only by the Pharisees, but in some of the schools in Sepphoris. She could speak and read Aramaic, Hebrew, Greek, Latin, and several of the other mid-eastern languages. She had always loved only Jesus, and had insisted that her family not marry her off to one of the sons of the local wealthy families. Because of her family's wealth and social position and, more importantly, her own intelligence and bearing, she avoided the mockery she might have felt at not being a wife and mother at her age. None dared confront her directly.

But she had known when Jesus had worked with his family renovating Martha's family's house in Sepphoris that she was in love. Jesus was well skilled in the building trade and could have become a well-respected, well-to-do tekton like his father, Joseph. After Joseph died, Jesus would join his brothers and the other workers in pursuing the trade his stepfather had taken over from his father. His building skills and training were readily apparent and permitted him to find work wherever in his travels he found himself.

As the young teenage girl, Mary watched Jesus, now in his mid-twenties, work. She followed him. He had dark, soulful eyes, heavy silken lashes, and eyebrows and a delicate hawk nose. His dark, curly hair hung about his shoulders. When, in repose and staring off in the distance while taking a break from his work, he looked like a deer. He had the thin body of an ascetic, but his early years in the building business had given him a wiry muscular build. As he was sitting with his back to the wall drinking from the jug, Mary would come up and sit beside him to discuss things. Their conversations ran through politics, history, the Torah and his travels. She was spellbound by his tales and insights, but could not help peppering him with questions about his travels and the other religions. His tales of exotic travels had her spellbound.

"Mary, leave him alone, let him work," her mother called. Her mother bore a shame among the women in the village that her beautiful niece entrusted to her care was not married in her mid-twenties. She was also too smart for her own good. She would scare off prospective husbands with her sharp wit and superior knowledge. Even though the family was wealthy and had an undeniable social position, the women of the village had to gossip. Any unseemly contact between her beloved Mary and an eligible man would make matters worse and lead to scandal. Mary, herself, could stare down any of the local gossip-mongers, but her mother had to live with a constant undercurrent of malicious chatter.

"Yes, mother." The eternal response of a child, no matter what age, to the scolding parent. Of course, she did not move and continued her conversation until Jesus had to return to work with his brothers.

Mary, as the daughter of a wealthy family, could in another society have been deemed to be a member of the aristocracy—although Jews held no such social distinctions. But she enjoyed the same rights and privileges. She was above the customs and mores of the lower class members of her sex. She was educated and was entitled to her opinion. She was not betrothed in a brokered marriage arranged by a go-between and the families of the bride and groom. Her unmarried status while an embarrassment to her aunt was a source of pride to her. She could choose her life and she chose Jesus.

In fact, she and several other women from wealthy families often gave money and other resources to Jesus and his disciples. Often, they followed him at a distance with appropriate creature comforts as his band went from small Galilean town to small town.

Now, Mary was prepared to press her case still further. She wanted to join Jesus' band as a disciple and travel where he went.

"Jesus, I want to be an Eshektal as in the Proverbs." She was referring to Proverb 31— a well known and oft-cited reference to the status of women in ordinary Jewish life.

Often, the wives of the disciples followed in Jesus' caravan and spent days and weeks on the road. Now Mary wanted to become one of those women. But she was not married to Jesus. It would certainly be a distraction from his message. Mary was living at the home of her uncle Joseph and his wife Leah, the parents of Mary's closest friend and cousin Martha. With Joseph away on one of his many business trips, the matriarch of the family Leah became the responsible elder for Mary, her deceased sister's niece. What could she do? Mary was a grown woman, but a walking scandal. This was a problem. Her niece living openly with a prominent holy man. Finally, Martha spoke up. "Mother, I could travel with Mary and live among the women in the camp."

"Aha, a chaperone." But what of Martha's husband? Fortunately, he was an understanding sort and an ardent follower of Jesus. If it would make the family happy, his wife could take a few trips here and there among the entourage, following Jesus to keep Mary's reputation and Jesus' image impeccable.

CHAPTER TWELVE

Lazarus and
Jesus Talk of Mandrake

"JESUS, CAN I SPEAK to you for a second?" Lazarus said. Jesus had known Lazarus since he was a young teenager. He was always wildly inventive. Fortunately, his family was well off and he could indulge most of his crazy notions. Mary Magalene and he were always apt to conspire to do something daring. Mary Magdalene's homage to maturity was to fall in love with Jesus, on whom she had first a puppy love crush and now a mature woman's adoration. Lazarus too had immediately been drawn to Jesus and often followed him on the stops throughout the Galilee.

"Of course, Lazarus. What's on your mind?"

"Well, I've been reading a lot lately and I spoke to a few men on a Persian caravan through here a few weeks ago. They have this mandrake mixture. What it does is make you look like you're dead for a few days and then you wake back up."

"Sounds dangerous."

"I thought so too, but I tried it on the red heifer in the shed over there. Sure enough, she fell right over. I had to cover her with straw so no one could see. She wasn't breathing and her eyes were rolled up in her head. I'd swear she was dead.

"Then, I came out about evening three days later and she was up and walking about like nothing happened."

"Still sounds dangerous." Jesus could feel some crazy idea about to pop and he didn't like where it was going.

"Well, suppose I gave it to someone really sick in a town and he looked dead for three days and then woke up. I mean if he was already so sick, it wouldn't matter if it didn't work out. Then we could know for sure. You could wake him up and everyone would think he had risen from the dead."

"Whoa! I don't like that one bit. Death is not something you play with, and these mandrakes can be poison. No, I don't like it."

"Just keep it in mind. In case something comes up."

CHAPTER THIRTEEN

Kaiaphas meets Pilate

KAIAPHAS WALKED SLOWLY AND painfully down Mule street past the vendor's shops until he ducked into the stall of the trader in fine linen goods from Tyre. Although he was only in his forties, he was covered in a disguise of an older storekeeper. It was considered a disgrace for a devout practicing Jew to enter the house of the Roman visitors. He also could not have it known that he was meeting unofficially with the Roman governor. As a result, he had to go to the meeting dressed as an elderly tradesman through a secret door in the rear of the yard goods store to meet Pilate. It was probably an unnecessary charade but one that Kaiaphas had to maintain to preserve the illusion that he was not totally subservient to the Romans.

The Sadducees had long held the right to hold the position of the high priests at the temple in Jerusalem for over a thousand years. They traced their lineage back to Aaron—Moses' brother—and to Zadok—from whose name the word Sadducees was derived. Originally, the twelve tribes included those of Levi but they were dispersed among the other ten tribes and the tribes of Ephraim and Manassa—two sons of Joseph were substituted in their place to complete the twelve tribes.

For years, the Sadducees had administered the many rites in the Hebrew temple. It had been a very profitable enterprise for them to control this franchise. The wealthy families who required a high priest to officiate at their bar mitzvahs, weddings, funerals were very amply compensated. In addition, the priesthood could levy a temple tax throughout the kingdom for the maintenance and care of the temple including of course their compensation as priests. They also sat and administered the courts where Jewish citizens could bring their disputes and enforce their grievances. The costs of these proceedings were also a lucrative source of income. They received fees for inspecting animals and products to ensure that they met the purity required in the Jewish dietary laws. In addition, they administered the sacrifices of anything from cattle and sheep to doves and grain and wine. The sacrifice of animals, once completed by being killed in a ritual manner and roasted over a flame in the temple compound, did not go to waste. The meat was distributed among the priestly families and, where appropriate, the poor. In short, the priesthood was an extremely well paid hereditary institution in Jewish life.

It was expected that the priestly families would be learned in the Torah and the other holy books of the Jewish tradition. They were expected to expound on Jewish law, Jewish history, and provide spiritual guidance in particular to the many local synagogues through not only the Israel and Judea but into the many lands to which the Jews had dispersed. Already there were Jewish settlements through the Middle East and Europe, particularly along the rivers and in the Mediterranean seaports where they traded in goods of all sorts. It was necessary that the reputation of the Sadducees be above reproach both as scholars of the Jewish tradition, but as moral leaders and examples to the entire Jewish people.

Under the Romans, this reputation was sorely tested. In keeping with its tradition, Rome insisted on being able to appoint the religious leaders of the various sects throughout its empire. It was not lost on the Romans that a religious leader who might cause them difficulties was a serious liability.

In the past with other conquered people, the Romans were able to control very easily the priests of the other cults, but the Jews were a problem. They were so different. They insisted with great rigidity on pursuing their own strange practices. They ate only certain foods, they had no statuary or art depicting humans and insisted their one God was superior to all others. And were willing to fight over these petty issues. Never before had a group been willing to fight with the Romans over its religious issues.

Where Pilate just came to Jerusalem to meet Kaiaphas, he was quick to assert his authority. He commanded Kaiaphas to come to Herod's palace and kept him and his entourage waiting for several hours. He then marched with a complement of 36 soldiers in full battle array along with the legion standard bearer into the courtroom. Herod Antipas then vacated his throne as Pilate mounted the steps and sat on the palace throne. He then conferred briefly with his clerk while Kaiaphas stood on the lower level. Finally, Pilate turned to Kaiaphas and said in latin. His words were interpreted for him into Aramaic.

"Priest! How do you call yourself!" Pilate well knew his name.

"Kaiaphas." He visibly stiffened at this slight affront of the assemblage in the court.

"And how long have you been high priest?" Again it was well known that this was a hereditary position, he had taken over from Annas his father-in-law. Kaiaphas had married the former priest's daughter.

"Four years," Kaiaphas answered in Greek—the language of the educated He repeated his answer in Latin as if Pilate might not understand Greek, but he kept a bland expression on his face.

"And how long do you intend to serve?" Again the words were interpreted to Aramaic. Again everyone knew that the Romans as part of their treaty had reserved the right to select the high priest.

"As long as I am able," Kaiaphas replied in Latin, dispensing with the Greek. Kaiaphas was well aware that the Romans could remove him at will and select a more compliant puppet to do their bidding. He did not wish to give, in public or this court setting, any cause for Pilate to seek his removal. On the other hand, he did not wish in public to appear to surrender completely his dignity and openly acknowledge the Roman authority to remove him. This ambiguous answer simply acknowledged reality. Obviously, a game was being played out where Kaiaphas would publicly have to acknowledge that his position rested on Roman authority, while being subtly defiant to a knowledgeable audience.

"How long is that you are able, priest?" No translation was offered.

"By the grace of God, your excellency." Again, an evasive ambiguity. He was implying he owed his fate to God and not the Romans.

"Whose god is that?"

"Why, of course, the one true God." He certainly wasn't going to concede that Caesar, who claimed to be divine, was a god. It was certainly safe to take refuge in his position as a religious leader of his own faith.

"Ah, the *true* god. The *one* god. Do you claim superiority over the Roman gods?"

"As you know, we believe our God is superior. We believe that He established a covenant with our people to be his chosen people and…"

"Let's not go into all that. Yes yes yes! Do you acknowledge the authority of Caesar in the governance of your land?" Pilate was careful under the rules of Roman rule not to demean or belittle the local religions.

"The terms of the treaty are clear."

"Do you intend to obey them?"

"If I am able." Kaiaphas was again ambiguous. He did not openly insist that where the terms of his religion contradicted Roman law, he would resist. Instead, he appeared to limit himself only to his physical ability, but was reserving the right to refuse to do so on moral or religious grounds.

"Do you know of any reason that you might not be able?"

"I see none." He clearly was using the latin present tense which did not concede future difficulties. It was obvious that he was avoiding the future tense—which could have suggested his intention to act in the future. This distinction was lost on all gathered in the courtroom except Kaiaphas and Pilate. It did not appear that any confrontation had taken place.

"Ah. But will you accept Roman authority?"

"By the grace of God, I hope that I will be able to do so." Again an evasion. Of course, the future was always unknown, and the Jewish laws might well interfere.

"Priest. Enough of this! Come into my chambers." Pilate abruptly left the court and exited through a door to the left. Kaiaphas followed.

Now, the meeting consisted only of Pilate, Kaiaphas, and their two clerks. Pilate did not know that Kaiaphas' clerk was his father-in-law Annas.

"Enough of these games, Kaiaphas. You know I am selecting your head priest—someone I will not have to play these petty games." It was Pilate who had staged the elaborate public spectacle.

"I am well aware of that, your excellency. I meant no disrespect."

"You had every opportunity to acknowledge that you were the proper candidate for the job."

"You must understand, your excellency, my public position is delicate. If I appear to be a Roman puppet, my people will not follow me or give me respect. Already, the Pharisees disparage our rank and position. Already they presume to perform rites which are rightly those only of the Sadducees. They blame our fortune to administer the religion on your conquest, as if it were a sign from God of our lack of piety. There are many preachers who condemn us and are jealous of our position. If you weaken our position you strengthen theirs." A clever ploy. He was insisting that the Romans support him as well as vice versa.

"As you know it is Rome's policy to permit you to administer your own laws and keep your religions. That is the central point of Pax Romana."

"But if I may be a bit indelicate, your excellency, we pay a large portion of our Temple tax to you and we receive the Temple tax from the people. If we cannot collect the appropriate tax from the people we cannot pay it over to you."

"We understand. I must be sure that you are the high priest we select who will make no waves. We want our taxes, we want you to keep the peace through the Jewish courts and we don't want you encouraging any rebellions or tactics against Romans. Is that clear?"

"I think we understand each other, but don't embarrass me in public. It is well known that I hold this position because I married the high priest's daughter. You should not appear to undermine my authority. You must understand my position. We Jews consider it wrong to enter the houses of those who do not practice our dietary laws. These laws are over a thousand years old. I cannot meet you at your palace, only at your courtyard. I also cannot recognize your Caesar as a god. That would be extremely sacrilegious. I can acknowledge that you can worship other gods, but not Caesar. There may be many things from time to time where you may wish to consult me to avoid creating an unnecessary provocation to my people. If you want peace and taxes, you should not stir the people with unintentional acts which contravenes their religious practices."

"I accept that point, but where can we meet?"

"My scribe will contact one of your people to arrange a safe site."

"Good. Let's leave it at that. Remember peace and taxes, and no trouble."

"I understand."

CHAPTER FOURTEEN

News of Lazarus' "Death"

JESUS AND THE ENTOURAGE had completed their ministry in the town of Exaloth and were plodding slowly back to their camp in the grove of olive trees at the hillside outside town. Some men and women were already sprawled on their blankets, while those appointed began to light the fire and chop the vegetables for the stew. Jesus sat on a rock and was fielding questions from some of the men. Off in the distance, they could see a cloud of dust and hear a voice shouting eagerly, "Master, master." The rider eventually drew up at the encampment and jumped off his donkey, lurching, stumbling and falling, he knelt before Jesus. He was the servant from Joseph's house in Bethany of Mary, Martha and Lazarus.

"Master, master, I bring news. Lazarus has fallen ill. You must come, the doctors can do nothing!"

Jesus shook his head and scratched at his beard slowly. "What does he look like?"

"He is lying still and doesn't seem to breathe."

"How did this happen, did he fall? Is there some illness in the village?"

"No. He was breaking his fast and then he just fell silent and leaned against a wall. That was this morning. I rode all the way."

"Mmm. I see. So that was this morning?"

"Yes, master."

"So, it is eight hours?"

"Yes, master."

"Very well, tell them I will come, but take some dinner first and stay with us tonight."

"But, master, he is ill."

"Yes. I understand. But stay. You cannot travel the Galilee at night."

The next morning, the servant and the entourage were up and rolling the gear, but looking over at Jesus for the next orders as to what they would do that day. Jesus was sitting on a rock, slowly eating his breakfast figs, and staring off into the middle distance.

Peter was the first who dared to approach him. "Master. Are we going to Bethany? Shouldn't we be packing the donkeys?"

"No. No...I think not. Today, we return to town and finish our ministry."

"But, master. What about Lazarus?"

"We will deal with him later."

"Very well." Peter returned to instruct the others that they were not traveling that day. A murmur arose, and the others asked "But what about this Lazarus?"

"The master says not yet. We stay here today."

All that day, the people looked over at Jesus with questioning looks but did not dare approach him. Jesus continued to answer the many questions from the assemblage as he usually did with stories or sermons. At the same time, he had his potions and an array of medicines spread out on the ground as people approached. He would listen to the complains and, on occasion, apply some medication. Again, by late afternoon, he retired back to the camp in the olive grove. Again, Peter approached him. "Master, do we go to Bethany tomorrow?" Again, Jesus shook his head slowly and finally answered. "Not yet, the day after." So that was it. By now everyone knew that Lazarus lay dying or dead and Jesus was doing nothing.

At first light the next day, the train was packed and ready as Jesus strode calmly up to his donkey and nodded to Peter. With that Peter shouted at the people and a procession began to queue up behind Jesus and Peter, and slowly wound their way out of town on the trail to Bethany. This would be a two day trip through the Galilee and Samaria to Bethany.

It was late in the second day and the sun was slowly beginning to disappear when a rider came up to the procession. "Master, you've come. But I fear too late. Lazarus died and was put in the tomb."

"Mmm. We must hurry then." Everyone turned and looked at each other, with puzzled looks. The caravan continued at a faster pace, but Jesus and Peter had their donkeys break into a trot. As they reached the sprawling complex of buildings, Martha came out to meet Jesus. "Where have you been? Lazarus died yesterday, you might have saved him." And she began to wail and keen, and scold Jesus.

Jesus said. "Bring me to him and bring Mary. Where is she?"

"She is grieving and mad at you."

"Bring her at once and meet me at the tomb."

As they approached the tomb, Mary came up on the run and began crying and shrieking. Her words were incomprehensible. Jesus grabbed her by the shoulders and hugged her. "Take me to him," was all he said.

As they approached the tomb, everyone crowded around to see what Jesus would do next.

"Roll back the stone." He commanded. Then Jesus came to the mouth of the burial cave and shouted. "Rise, Lazarus, and come forth." A simple command. A stirring was heard from inside and then a figure clad in the burial wrappings appeared at the door. He staggered slightly and held his eyes against the light. As he peeled off the wrappings, Lazarus emerged. The crowd gasped and chattered nervously. Lazarus was back. Jesus had recalled him from the dead without a prayer, without any ritual. Just a simple command.

Mary and Martha ran to him and began to touch his hands and arms tentatively. With tears running down their cheeks they hugged him and squeezed him. More tears. More shrieks. Jesus remained calm and said nothing. This went on for half an hour, until Martha and Mary led Lazarus back into the house. "Prepare some lentil soup. He must be starved." Lazarus limped and supported by both women, went into the house. The realization was beginning to dawn on the people: Jesus had raised Lazarus from the dead! It was a miracle beyond question. The crowd lingered to the early morning hours, while the family remained inside. Jesus and his group bedded down in their usual Bethany site in the orchard after a meal brought out by the servants. The local Pharisees were already huddling and whispering. What had this Jesus done and so close to Jerusalem. This was not the Galilee with a countryside full of poor peasants. They were in Judea four miles from Jerusalem.

The next day Lazarus and Mary Magdalene came out to see Jesus. The three went off a good distance from the camp. When they were well out of earshot, Jesus turned abruptly on Lazarus.

"That was reckless and stupid. And you scared everyone to death. What made you do this?"

Lazarus with head held down said "Jesus, I am sorry. I told you about the gall but you didn't believe me. So I went to the Persians in Jaffa and they showed me: the exact doses, the body weight, the length of sleep. It all worked. I swear I saw it before my own eyes. I swear it."

Mary Magdalene at first stood there with her eyes wide. "You did what? You imbecile. You idiot." Words flooded out, some without sound, some in a screech. "You almost killed yourself. You let us have a funeral. We buried you. We grieved. Do you know what you did? What were you thinking?" As she did this, she hit him with her fists on his arms and chest, crying blubbering, spilling out words.

Jesus glared at Lazarus. "I told you not to. It was too dangerous."

"But Jesus, I thought if you raised me from the dead, it would be a great miracle and everyone would believe."

"I don't need miracles. I don't want miracles. This does nothing except for the ignorant. It is not a true conversion. They will expect miracles everytime, and then they will fight over who got miracles and who didn't. Miracles are meaningless. It is the soul of men I seek. People who look for cheap miracles will never believe in the true doctrine. They seek only the physical, not the spiritual. They must recreate the world by themselves, with true repentance and obedience. Otherwise, it is a hollow belief. One for fickle people only. Don't you understand? I don't want cheap conversions, I want real ones. Besides, miracles only heal a few, good doctrine must convert the many."

"I see, Master." To Lazarus, it was clear Jesus was not talking as a friend but as a holy man.

"You have unleashed problems, I don't think I can control. The Sadducees don't believe in resurrection, the Pharisees only see the soul may be resurrected at the end of days. Now, we have met death and resurrected you. Why do you deserve to be resurrected, because I love you and your family? No. My ministry is for everyone who believes in the one God, not just my friends. Some may see through your little trick and blame me as a charlatan and a fraud.

"Now, they will believe I have blasphemed. They will suspect me of magic and sorcery rather than true belief. Don't you see? It has created too many problems. It has created jealousy and suspicion. If you found the gall, the Pharisees will learn about it as well. No. It was a stupid stunt and you almost died."

Mary listened with her mouth agape and wide-eyed. "You mean you took something to make you look dead?"

Lazarus, by this time, was crying. "I'm sorry. I thought it would help."

"Help? Help? What could you have been thinking? Everyone mourning! And the danger—you could have died and for what, for a phony miracle." She was just getting started. Finally Jesus grabbed her and stroked her back.

"Mary; Mary! The boy is young and he meant well. I have not taught him enough. It is over, thank God; but we must clean up the mess. Calm down. The others must not know and we must instruct others not to tell what happened. I cannot draw inquiries. There are many jealous of my ministries and I don't need more enemies. Now, let us go back and instruct everyone to keep silent about what has occurred here." Mary calmed down to small whimpers and began to nod in comprehension. She and Jesus looked with darts at Lazarus.

"I know I know. I'll obey. You can count on me."

BOOK TWO

CHAPTER ONE

Jesus' Entry into Jerusalem

LAZARUS AND THE OTHERS had already chosen the hillside of Gethsemane to bed down for the night. It was only a half hour's walk to the Susa Gate and directly across the valley from the Temple. The site was an olive grove and there was a large stone press around the trees. The owner, a good friend of Joseph of Arimathea, had let Jesus' company have it for the coming Passover festival. In a few days, the population of Jerusalem would swell from 25,000 to 250,000 from the pilgrims coming in from all over. Several of the disciples had preceded Jesus and the main group to the site and secured it from the hordes pouring over the hills to Jerusalem.

Jesus had arranged for a grand entrance into Jerusalem, and it was hoped that he would draw a large crowd. The entry of the messiah had been foretold in Ezekiel. "Rejoice greatly, O daughter of Zion, shout O daughter of Jerusalem, behold thy king cometh unto thee; he is just and having salvation, lowly and riding upon an ass." Jesus had carefully instructed his followers to procure all the necessary ingredients to fulfill the prophecy.

He had obtained a small donkey and its colt and rode it down the Kidron Valley to enter the Water Gate. His disciples and followers had stored up a number of palm fronds for a large group of followers who began to throw the fronds in front of the donkey and sing "Hosanna, hosanna!" as he entered the gate. A crowd started to form. The Roman sentries came to attention.

Unfortunately, the entrance through the gate lead directly past the Temple Mount where large numbers of Roman guards had been posted along the route. It had been near that site that the Zealots including Judas, Simon, and Thaddeus and the rest of the Jerusalem cell had staged a revolt against Pilate over a year earlier. Even now they were being sought for this insurrection, but had escaped into the hills. The Romans correctly assumed that they would return to Jerusalem in the guise of pilgrims and create more mischief during the holiday weekend when they city would be gorged with pilgrims for the Passover.

The revolt had been staged to protest Roman corruption. Pontius Pilate had been using funds collected by the Temple to have his personal water supply improved. When a formal complaint was lodged against him in court, the Roman soldiers murdered the complainants and an uproar ensued immediately. It had not been designed as a truly military event, but more of an embarrassing protest. During the course of the protest, some of the Zealots had sought to provoke the soldiers further and the entire affair had resulted in a rather bloody suppression. The leaders of the uprising were of course vigorously sought.

Secretly, Herod Antipas had delighted in the anger Pontius Pilate had caused and hoped that his heavy handed tactics in preserving the Pax Romana would reach Rome. He further instigated the rebels in their uprising and had them kept apprised of the Roman maneuvers to quell the latest outburst. At the appropriate time, Antipas had a few of his men disguised as protesters kill a few of the Roman soldiers. While Pilate had survived this embarrassment to his regime, it had continued to make him extremely sensitive to any incendiary activity among the Jews and this Passover was not a time for him to rest. As a result, he marched from Caesarea into Jerusalem at the head of two Roman legions in full battle regalia including tubas and trumpets with the soldiers beating their swords on their shields.

As a result the well-known prediction from Zechariah 9:9 was fulfilled by a "king riding on a donkey through the Water Gate into Jerusalem" but lightly attended. Jesus' heritage of descent from David was unmistakable. This symbolic act of humility and signified his accessibility to the lowest of his subjects. But the residents of Jerusalem and surrounding Judea paid little attention or were somewhat amused by Jesus. He was from Galilee and considered a leader only of country bumpkins. His very speech with the Galilean accent—even if now slight—would draw a few giggles as he tried to express his religious zeal. Only his fellow Galileans were attracted to his teachings.

As the procession on the donkey wound through the streets, many of the curious inhabitants observed this newcomer from Galilee ride through their town, past the menacing glances of the Roman soldiers, and under the windows of Antipas, and Pilate. The game was on.

Somewhat dispirited by the low turnout and favorable but polite attention, Jesus had his followers dissipate through the streets and filtered back through the city gates and over the valley to Gethsemane.

Jesus sat staring and silent for some time against a tree in the olive grove. The disciples knew better than to talk to him now, but they sat silently around him and waited for him to speak. One of the women brought him a bowl of lentils. Eventually, he began to pick at the bowl.

"Master…" Peter began, but Jesus raised his hand softly and shook his head. He got up and went to the far end of the encampment where he knelt in prayer.

At last, he stood up and returned to the disciples. "Tomorrow is another day."

CHAPTER TWO

Beggar Announces Arrival of Jesus to Pilate

THERE WAS A CLATTER and some shouting down the hallway as the two soldiers dragged a disheveled street person into the Praetorium.

"Get your hands off me! I have news. His excellency will want to hear me and will pay me handsomely. You'll regret not showing me respect." The man tumbled on the floor before the guards.

"Get up, you vermin and move along."

Pontius Pilate and several of the courtiers looked at the hallway where the noise was coming from. The Procurator Pilate was in the midst of hearing a dispute between a tax collector and a wealthy merchant. The merchant had brought his scribe and several witnesses. Scattered about the tables were receipts and bills of lading in piles as the argument over the taxes changed as several shipments were being discussed.

A tall Roman centurion came to the entrance of the praetorium and saluted. He was dressed in full battle array except for the plumed helmet. He still wore the gilded leather chestplate, and maroon battle uniform.

"Yes. Marcus Gracilus, what is it?" Consul Pilate knew the soldier would not interrupt this court session without good reason. He was a trained official and well knew the dangers of bothering the consul with trivial matters, especially when he was busy with matters involving money.

"A man from the Water Gate says we had a new visitor to the city that we should pay some attention. I wouldn't have…"

"Oh very well." He turned the assembled court and addressing the merchant and his scribe, apologized. "I'm sorry. This seems to be a matter of some importance. I'll have to adjourn until tomorrow." Then turned to the chief clerk, "At when?"

"Your excellency has ten to noon open unless you have something else planned."

"No. No. That's fine. We will resume at ten o'clock tomorrow."

The litigants slowly gathered up their scrolls and put them into large leather carrying bags and made for the door.

"Not that door, please leave by the other door!"

After all the litigants had left the room, the consul turned to the chief clerk. "Leave us and get Generals Gallicus and Asclipio up here as soon as you can." As the clerk left, the consul turned to the Gracilus. "Bring in this man. Let's hear what he has to say in the antechamber." Pilate left in the opposite direction.

Two soldiers each grabbing a spindly arm of a thoroughly scared street person, dragged the beggar to the antechamber. Soon Pilate appeared dressed in the robes of a scribe. The beggar had on only a filthy robe covered with grease stains and his thick matted black hair hung in greasy tendrils. Pilate took a seat quietly next to the generals, as if he were merely a bureaucrat recording the session

"Your worshipful excellency, I have news of a valuable nature…"

"Silence. I want others to hear this tale! It had better be the truth or you will pay dearly for this interruption…"

"But…your excellency…the Nazarene from Galilee…"

"I said, silence! We'll hear your story when Consuetius has come and not before. Keep your mouth shut until then."

"But…your excellency…!"

The centurion behind him hit him with the butt of his spear and sent the fellow tumbling forward onto the marble floor. He rolled over slowly and got to his feet, looking warily behind him.

Soon, Consuetius, Pilate's man in charge of strategy against the rebels came through the doors and saluted. Gallicus spoke first. "We heard you had some information." They looked over at the cowering figure in the filthy robe. "Is this he?"

"Yes. I wanted all of us to hear what he says is so 'valuable.' How valuable is this news you bring us? It had better be good. You have interrupted an entire afternoon of court time. Now, out with it."

Consuetius and the Generals moved to the benches on the side of the court, and forced the figure who now crouched in the middle of the room and looked at the military personnel surrounding him.

"I swear it is as good as gold. I have seen it myself. He came in the Water Gate…"

"Who? Who came in the Water Gate?"

"The Nazarene from the Galilee. The preacher…he came in riding a donkey through the Water Gate. They were throwing palm fronds and singing hosanna."

"Whoa. Whoa. Which preacher?"

"Jesus and his disciples. They came in the Water Gate and he was riding a donkey."

"Who was riding the donkey?"

"Jesus, the preacher. He was riding a donkey just as it says in Isaiah."

"Who is Isaiah?"

"Isaiah. Our great prophet. We read his story in the haftorah."

"Slow down. Where is this Isaiah?"

"He's dead. He's been dead."

"Who killed him? How did he die?"

"No. No. No. He's one of our great prophets. He died over six hundred years ago. We read his story now in the haftorah."

"I've heard of the Torah, but now you have a haftorah. What is that?"

"Moses wrote the Torah. Then after he died, the scribes kept an account of our history from there. They told the stories of David and Solomon, of the Judges and the prophets for a thousand years."

"Alright. Alright. And what of Isaiah?"

"He was our greatest prophet. But he foretold that the messiah would come riding into the Water Gate in Jerusalem on a donkey."

"When did he say this?"

"Over six hundred years ago."

"Who reads this haftorah?"

"We all do. Once a year we read every part of the haftorah. We read Isaiah and we also read the Midrash."

"You mean everyone reads?"

"Mostly everyone, except the women and many of them read some. Every male has to read his torah and haftorah portions on the day he is a bar mitzvah."

"But every male knows this story."

"Yes excellency. We all do. We hear it once a year."

"We've heard of this preacher, but he has a large following and he preaches all over Galilee."

"Why has he come to Jerusalem. It's Passover. Everyone that can, comes to the Temple."

"Yes. Yes I know that, but why on a donkey? If he has such a large following and he is coming in for the Passover, why is he riding a donkey. He must look like a dirt farmer."

"Well. He does preach that worldly goods and worldly comforts are not important."

"Alright, but why not walk? Why a donkey?"

"It was prophesied that the messiah would come into Jerusalem riding a donkey on Passover."

"What is a messiah?"

"One anointed to lead the people in times of trouble."

Pilate looked at the Generals who shrugged back in reply. They came up and began to whisper with Pilate. Eventually, one of the Generals turned to the beggar, tossed him a few coins and shouted at him. "That's enough, beggar, now begone." With that the two guards on either side hoisted him up by his arms and dragged him from the room.

As they approached the east door of the Palace, they tossed him out onto the street.

CHAPTER THREE

Zebediah Reports to Zealots

ZEBEDIAH THE BEGGAR WALKED out of the marketplace from Pilate's headquarters with his limp becoming less noticeable. He looked at his hand and found he was several shekels richer. As he continued to look over his shoulder and stopped at a number of stalls in the market place. He waited until he was sure no one was following him. Eventually he ducked into a butcher shop and went to the rear, opened a door in the rear and came into a small room with three men eating hummus and drinking tea. "Done," he said, "all done and I got a few shekels into the bargain." He took off the greasy keftan and threw it in the corner and crouched over a large bowl of water wiping his face, arms and chest free of the grime caked on. "Oh, damn, I cannot get rid of this manure smell, and I hope I never see that robe again!"

Bar Abbas was the first to speak. "So, Zebediah, tell us everything in detail and don't leave anything out."

"First, they wouldn't let me in, but I told them someone was attracting a large crowd and I had to speak to his excellency the Procurator at once. The stupid guards just shooed me away but the big German centurion overheard. When I explained to him, he seemed to know all about Jesus and he grabbed me by the arm and dragged me in. I told him all about the donkey and Isaiah. They seemed not to know, but they did give me the coins and let me go."

"So now they know," said Simon. "The game is on. They asked you about Isaiah?"

"Oh, yes. I explained he was a prophet and described the Messiah who would enter Jerusalem from the Water Gate. The whole megillah. They just looked at each other. Maybe they knew, maybe they didn't. Now, they do."

"Well, it's up to them. What can they do? He hasn't committed a crime, but he has drawn a crowd during Passover. What will they do? And how will they explain it to Rome? Did he look concerned?"

"I couldn't tell. He called for his two Generals, Gallicus and Asclipio before he heard me. And Gallicus, the big one was standing over me. He was careful to include the chief clerk of the court session before I said anything. So, it was just the military, the clerk and me. He didn't seem to want anyone else to know about me."

"He didn't have his legal consultant?

"No, just the two Generals, the clerk and me, all in the antechamber."

"That's not good. We need to have him think about the criminal issue, not just the military one. He might do something stupid. We need to get him to think this through and not commit some new outrage. He knows Rome is concerned about his previous acts and doesn't want any new trouble. This incidents about the Temple money being used for the aqueduct must make him think twice before he acts. Rome might recall him if he pulls another outrage.

"Remember that Samaritan incident, too. He is on his last legs if he blows this one."

CHAPTER FOUR

Pilate and the Generals Confer

A S SOON AS THE beggar left, Pilate looked at the two generals, "What was that? Who is he talking about?"

"It's that Galilean preacher. We've had him watched for months. He attracts large crowds when he speaks in the towns near Galilee. He seems harmless," said Gracches; "although, he could be a problem, a crowd could turn ugly when we have everyone in from the countryside for this Passover business."

"Who is he? What's he saying?"

"He seems to be preaching reform of the Jewish church. He sounds a bit like a Pharisee, but he seems to dispute with them too. He wants greater attention to their laws. He sounds like one of their old prophets and seems to be preaching a traditional Jewish theme of repentance and a return to their old ways. I don't hear any revolutionary claims."

"I don't understand what does their God have to do with this and who are the Pharisees?"

"Well, you have to understand these people. They're a strange group. They believe about 1,200 years ago, their god rescued them from slavery in Egypt and gave them this land which is the area of Judea and Israel. You remember, our jurisdiction is Judea and Herod's is Galilee. Believe me, you got the better of the deal. You don't want northern territory. That region around Galilee is a wild, ungovernable land. The Babylonians, Assyrians, the Samaritans, and every other imaginable group, all wander through in their caravans.

There are many bandits from many different tribes that attack the caravans and the travelers. Many of the zealots hide in the caves and farm houses. Galilee split from Judea years ago."

"But, about this preacher, is he Galilean?"

"By birth, yes. His father was tekton near Sepphoris. About four miles away is the town of Nazareth where he comes from."

"Is he a zealot?"

"I don't think so, but many zealots follow him. They may be working on him to lead a movement. So far, he only seems to have influence in Galilee, and so far, he only seems to be a preacher."

"What do we do now?"

Pilate walked over to the window and stared out at the Temple for several minutes. The generals stood silent and looked at each other.

"Follow him and see what he does and who he talks to."

"All right, where is he staying?"

"He and his people are camped over in Gethsemane across the Kidron Valley. He has about fifteen people with him. They don't seem to be armed. He has been seen with one of the Sicarii. For what reason we don't know."

"What do the Jews think of him?"

"We don't know yet. The people from Judea regard Galileans as their stupid country cousins. They laugh at the Galilean accent. But most of the leaders of rebellions over the years have come from Galilee. He could be one of them."

"Get that…what's his name…Kaiaphas over here. We agreed to permit him to be high priest. He runs the Sanhedrin. He owes us. We'll find out what's going on."

"I hear you and take your counsel, General," Pilate said. "But I need to know more." He pulled the bell cord by his chair. Almost instantly, his manservant came in.

"Yes, your excellency."

"Get me Kaiaphas. And don't take anything from him. I want him here now!"

"Yes, your excellency." And hurried out of the Praetorium.

CHAPTER FIVE

Kaiaphas Meets with Pilate

K AIAPHAS AS THE HIGH priest was extremely busy with the preparations for Passover. With over 250,000 people trying to get their burnt offerings and then be blessed by the priests it was like a madhouse. Then there was the whole Passover seder.

Within the hour, Kaiaphas along with his chief clerk, who was in disguise, his father-in-law and former chief priest, Annas, came into the Antonia Palace accompanied by six Roman soldiers. Kaiaphas had been interrupted in his duties at the Temple a short fifty meters away and was somewhat flustered by the insistence on his public appearance before Pilate. Although he had come to the Praetorium, he was asked to wait in the small antechamber for an hour before Pilate arrived accompanied by two Generals. Kaiaphas rose as Pilate took his seat in the antechamber.

"Priest! Who is this Jesus that comes through the Water Gate with such ceremony?"

"Your excellency, he is a preacher from Galilee. He is very popular up there."

"Does he have armed followers? Is he interested in rebellion?"

"I don't know much about him except that he has many religious followers. I don't believe he has any military experience or training."

"What does he preach?"

"As I am told, he claims to preach greater devotion to our laws and love of his fellow man." He was careful to avoid the term messiah. That would be too difficult to explain.

"Love of his fellow man! What is this?"

"I am not sure. I intend to look into this more deeply."

"Does he claim any dynastic rights?"

"They say he is descended from the legacy of David. David as you may not know was our much beloved king about one thousand years ago. But many claim descent from David. It's been nearly fifty generations. He had eight wives and many concubines. His heir Solomon had over nine hundred wives and concubines. Over one thousand years, there has been much intermarriage. Many people can claim some link to David. As far as the Maccabees, no, there is no connection."

The Hasmoneans were the most recent dynasty. They derived from the Maccabees—a family that had led a revolt against the Assyrians and procured freedom for the state of Judah about one hundred and fifty years prior. However, they squandered their chance as an independent state by murdering each other for access to the throne. Eventually, two competing parties to the throne sought assistance from Rome and were greeted by the Roman army who marched bloodlessly into Judea and took over the country without much resistance. The Hasmoneans had long ago worn out their welcome and were no longer popular.

"I want no trouble from this Jesus. Do you understand, no trouble. None. Once his crowd turns hostile, you must take action. I want no trouble during your feast day. What is it called?"

"Passover."

"During Passover. No trouble. We have over 250,000 people in this city for your feast day and I want no trouble. I will have my men watching him, and I want your guard on him as well. Do you hear?"

"Yes, I understand."

CHAPTER SIX

Spy tells of Judas

IT WAS ABOUT AN hour's ride north from Jerusalem, the scrofulous Egyptian sat at the feet of the large man sitting on the rock by the side of the road. The large man was, in fact, Aegilus, the aide to the Roman general Asclipio. "I've seen him. I'm sure." The Egyptian blurted out. "I have followed him as you wanted and I am sure."

"Well, what have you seen?"

"This man is Judas, he is a Sicarii and a zealot. I have followed him through the streets of Jerusalem and into the hills near Bethlehem. He makes regular contact with the zealots."

"Many people make contact with many people. So what?"

"I have seen him in the company of these zealots, and I have seen his knife—it is a sicar. No doubt."

"Well what then?"

"I have seen him travel to this Jesus, bringing donkeys laden with food. He has several other zealots acting as guards. He delivers these goods to Jesus and his followers. No doubt. No doubt.

"This Judas speaks with a Judean accent. I have heard him. He is not like the others—the Galileans. He is educated, and wears fancy robes, but he is a Zealot."

"So you claim Jesus and his Galileans are connected to the zealots through this man Judas, who is a Judean."

"No doubt, no doubt." The Egyptian was rocking back and forth, with his eyes cast warily upward at the general. Would he be believed and rewarded or spurned and whipped?

Aegilus stared off into the middle distance. Other spies had told him of this Judas making deliveries to Jesus and his group. He was definitely a Judean and spoke with an educated Judean accent. Unlike the rest of Jesus' followers, he was not from Galilee and did not have that accent. And now, he was a zealot or a sicarii. This was too much. He would need more corroboration but this was valuable. Of course, he couldn't betray to this man any interest or surprise. The price might go up and he might seek money from the zealots to tell a story to them of his interest. He must feign disinterest. "You tell me nothing. Who are these zealots he sees, where are they? Give me some names! Where do they live? I can't use this."

"But master, you told me what you wanted. I gave it to you."

"Yes. You gave me what you knew I wanted to hear."

"But it is true. No doubt. No doubt."

"Get me more." With that, he threw a bag of coins at the Egyptian and strode off back to Jerusalem.

CHAPTER SEVEN

Moneychangers

PANDEMONIUM BROKE OUT FROM all quarters. In the calm of the Praetorium where Pilate was sitting, six large and beefy soldiers sprang from along where they stood guard at the walls to surround Pilate's seat with their shields up and their spears extended. All around horns blew. The Roman tubas on the roof of Antonia Castle had probably sounded first as the soldiers on the roof ran to the side which overlooked the Temple courtyard. The Temple guards sounded their horns and rushed into the courtyard with swords drawn. The crowd in the courtyard began to scream and panic in a stampede for the doorway. But loudest may have been the merchants and animals in the courtyard who bleated and cried—running in their cages. What was happening?

Pilate rose in his chair and turned to the Centurion of his guard. "Find out what this is, at once.' The Centurion was out of earshot before Pilate finished his command.

Meanwhile, the Temple priests burst through the doors to the sanctuary to see what the commotion was about. The lines of people with their animals, the lines waiting to buy animals, the lines waiting to change money all were in upheaval. 25,000 stuffed into the outer court of the Temple began to jostle and shout. Something was happening, but what?

And the people, the animals, the doves scattered and ran into or over each other emitting a cacophony of human and animal noises—all indistinguishable. The animals bolted, squealed, urinating and defecating as they leaped and struggled against the pilgrims' twines. People began to run in all directions, clutching their money, dragging animals, all squealing and shouting. It was pandemonium.

In the midst of the noise and tumult was Jesus. Jesus alone surrounded by a number of husky Galilean fisherman as he swept through the large courtyard, overturning tables and shouting curses.

"A den of thieves! This is an abomination! You have made this holy place a den of thieves!"

It was mid morning and the courtyard was the most crowded at that time. Jesus had interrupted many transactions with many people and many animals. Of course, a main function of the Temple was to perform the rite of sacrifice of cattle, lambs, chickens, dove, as well as grain and wine. The items for sacrifice had to be "pure," ritually pure, acceptable for sacrifice to God. Since most of the pilgrims had come many miles, they could not be expected to bring their animals with them and were required to purchase these special animals locally. However, Jews would not permit these animals to be purchased with unholy coins, but only Judean shekels. Coins were unholy if they bore the image of a human or at worse a human ruler who asserted that he was divine. They were forced to change their foreign coin for Judean shekels which usually bore images of grapes, or grain or other inanimate objects. The moneychangers and animal sellers charged huge commissions for these transactions which they shared with the Temple priests. In all, Passover was a very happy and lucrative time for the priests, and the merchants.

But the courtyard where these financial and agricultural transactions took place was a massive open-air market. It had masses of people dragging all manner of animals who in fear and consternation were emitting sounds, excrement and odors of many sorts. The aisles were crowded and redolent. The people and the merchants yelled and haggled just above the braying, lowing, squealing and screeching of the animals. The city swelled during Passover from 25,000 people to over 250,000 and half of that number was in or crowding to get into the courtyard. It was the most crowded, fetid, noisy market in the known world in its busiest week.

Into this chaos had come Jesus and a cadre of club-wielding Galileans shouldering people aside while Jesus shouted and overturned the aisles, smashed the cages, and generally disrupted the scene.

It took little time for the Roman soldiers overlooking the courtyard or the Temple guards surrounding the courtyard to realize something was amiss, but it took longer to focus on this group of rampant Galileans.

By that time, they had all exited from a different gate and dispersed among the narrow streets of the city. Chaos, confusion, panic, perturbation reigned in their wake and then they were gone.

Eventually the Temple guards restored order, smacking pilgrims and animals with the sides of their swords and bellowing out orders. As the noise subsided, the high priests of the Temple appeared at the top of the Temple stairs. The heads of the Temple guards hastened up to them and began to explain what had happened. After a lengthy back and forth with the guards, Annas and Kaiaphas started directly for the Palace next door with an entourage of Temple guards. The procession walked in the open foyer in front of the Palace. It would have made the priests ritually impure—especially in public—to enter the house of a Roman gentile so they patiently waited outside on Pilate's pleasure.

Pilate took little time responding this time. This was a perilous time. The city was swelled with pilgrims, he had ordered most of his legions east to Jerusalem from Caeseria to discourage any mischief and he was in no mood to suffer any mischief this day.

Before the priests could start their ponderous explanation, Pilate demanded, "What's the meaning of this?"

"Your excellency, it seems this preacher from Galilee…"

"Galilee! That snakepit. What hell has come to us from Galilee?"

"Well this preacher is disrupting our courtyard. He is scattering the moneychangers and abusing the animals…"

"Why! …Why would he do that?"

"From what we understand, he thinks it is impious to change money or sell animals in the Temple courtyard."

"Uh-huh. And you sacrifice these animals as we do?"

"Yes…but."

"And your priests get their charred meat, just as ours do."

"Well, yes."

"And you profit from this money changing and animal selling?"

"Yes...but."

"And he thinks this is wrong?"

"Yes."

"So he has interfered with your business and your finances."

"That's true...but."

"So, it seems this is a big problem for you during this week. Especially this week."

"Yes..."

"A big problem for you. Why a problem for me?"

"He claims to be a messiah and he is attracting followers."

"What's a messiah?"

"One who is anointed as a leader."

"Uh...huh...a leader."

With that, Pilate sat on a nearby stone bench, mulling. "A leader, a messiah." Then he jerked up, abruptly. "All right, be gone. Let me think about this!" He swirled around and left the foyer followed by his guard. The priests looked at each other, each questioning the other. What had just happened? What was Pilate going to do?

Meanwhile, a general buzz had run through the city. "This Galilean...Jesus...from where?...did what?...right under the priests' noses...I saw it myself...what? A den of thieves...Oh, the Sadducees must love that, those greedy mongers!...On Passover, ha ha. Good one!...That guy knows his oats!...what are they going to do?... Especially that Roman toady, Kaiaphas...Maybe they'll cut the prices..."

Once back in Kidron Valley, Jesus and the men assembled. Jesus was excited and trembling. Peter said. "Let them ignore us now. We got their attention!" The men cheered and slapped one another on the back. It had been a good day.

CHAPTER EIGHT

Judas' Arrest

INSIDE THE ANTONIA PALACE, Judas was pushed onto the floor of one of the inner chambers. He had been beaten and tortured and now he stood before Gallicus, the general.

"Are you the Iscariot?"

Judas sat on the floor and continued to look dazed. He knew there was no answer to these questions and that he must die in the end.

"Are you a zealot?"

Again, no answer.

"Do you know this Jesus from Galilee?"

Again, no answer. Several questions more, followed by silence. False answers, smart answers were useless. They seemed to know already.

"We can tell by your accent you are a Judean. Why do you consort with this Jesus?

"Were you in the riots of last year with Bar Abbas?" Some informant must have already given them answers.

"Will you testify against this Jesus?" The general knew they needed two witnesses for a court trial either under the Roman laws or Jewish law. Absurd that they thought he might cooperate. Even if he did, he would forever be a marked man among the Jews for his cooperation. He well knew that any cooperation would be reported by his own spies back to the sicarii who killed Jewish collaborators with Rome. Silence and death were his only options.

The general had tonight's arrest of Jesus planned for some time and it would have to occur that night, after the Passover feasts.

There was no time for more beatings and torture. He would have to bring Judas to the arrest, and discredit Judas before his people.

"Bring this man to the Water Gate and clean him up. Let him go back to this Jesus. Tell him after the Passover feast he must come back to us or we will slaughter his family."

Judas was pulled up to a standing position and shoved out the door. After the door slammed behind him, he looked back. He knew he was doomed and Jesus was doomed.

CHAPTER NINE

Judas Reports to Jesus

JUDAS WENT TO THE second floor room where Joseph of Arimathea had arranged for the Passover feast for Jesus and the disciples. As the men trundled into the room, they walked past tables where the dishes for the feast lay in wait. As Jesus entered, Judas rose and hastened to Jesus. "Master, I must speak with you."

"Of course, Judas, what is it?"

"Master, I have been captured and interrogated. I was in the cellar of the Antonia Palace when you were in the Temple Court with the moneychangers. I have been there for two days. I told them nothing of course, but they seem to know all about me and you. They seem to have been following me for some time and see that I deliver provisions to you and your followers. They were very concerned that I spoke with a Judean accept and you and your people were Galileans. They think we are plotting some joint revolt with the Judean Zealots and your Galileans."

"What do they know?"

"They have taken Bar Abbas and others into custody. They will probably crucify them on Passover. Someone has told them of the revolt this past year and they know we are the Zealots involved. Someone must have informed. They seem to have gotten us all."

"Ah, not good!"

"But then they have followed me!"

"And?"

"They have seen me delivering provisions and money to your camp for some time now. They think you might be one of us."

"Us who?"

"Us the Zealots. They think because of me, you are connected to some Zealot activity, especially on Passover. I'm sorry, master, I seem to have betrayed your mission. I know you have said you will not join the Zealots, but you may have been thrown in with us anyway."

"We must keep this from the others. I want to have a proper Passover service and I want them to learn from this."

"Master, you could run. ...Go back to Galilee and continue your ministry. Take the others, save them."

"No. I would never be believed again. I must confront the Romans in a trial before the people. Surely, no one can prove anything against me. It would be a lie."

"The Sadducees have great power with the Romans and you disrupted the Temple Court yesterday. I heard all about it. Kaiaphas was called before Pilate and was no doubt told to keep the peace at all costs."

"Only the Sanhedrin can do anything to me, and the Sadducees are only part of the Sanhedrin. I have friends on the Sanhedrin among the Pharisees and the scribes. I have done nothing under Jewish law to be punished for. I have committed no blasphemy, I came to fulfill the law, not to destroy it. Besides, they will need two witnesses, two eyewitnesses, to testify against me. They can't have any. No. I'm not afraid of the Sadducees."

"But the Romans. They could crucify you like Bar Abbas. They can ignore their own laws and crucify you because they just don't like you."

"But what do they know? That you—a Zealot—bring me grain and donations. That can't be a crime. I have no weapons, no military training. We are a poor band of itinerant preachers."

"They have heard you are the messiah."

"From whom?"

"Many say this."

"Those are their words, not mine."

"Oh, Jesus. I know these men. They are not like Jews. The law is not sacred to them. Murder, crucifixion, idolatry, it is part of their life. They can do as they please."

"I will ask for a public trial. I know my rights. Rome must honors its own laws."

"I fear for you, Jesus. These Romans are barbarians."

"Let me worry about that."

The men from the other room were shuffling about now. The Passover feast was waiting. Jesus and Judas joined the others. They sat around the table. Mary Magdalene was the only woman and she sat to Jesus' right—the place of honor.

The service started. Prayers and stories about the escape of the Jews from slavery in Egypt—the Exodus.

As the meal progressed, Jesus began to sift through what Judas had told him. Yes, he might be killed, crucified by the Romans, as a suspected Zealot. What would become of his followers—would they continue his ministry as he had John's just a few years ago? Why had he been so bold as to come to Jerusalem, especially during Passover? He believed God would support him and his mission because it was holy. Now was to come a world of peace and justice. Yes. Now.

Jesus rose and addressed the followers. "Take this wine, it will be in remembrance of my blood, take this unleavened bread, it will be in remembrance of my body." Jesus was beginning to face the realization that he might die.

The men of the table were a bit dumbfounded. Could Jesus somehow be talking about his death? But Jesus said so many strange things they could not understand, this must mean something. But what?

Jesus then said "One of you must betray me tonight." Without looking at Judas, he continued, "Better to go on your mission. It must be carried out." The men were immediately in an uproar, what could this mean? Betrayal? How so? Who was it? What would they do? But Jesus had that faraway look on his face. As so many times before, he was saying something strange. Maybe when he had stopped this intense concentration, he would explain.

Judas slipped quietly out the side door.

CHAPTER TEN

March Across Kidron Valley. Jesus' Arrest

THE CENTURION BARKED TO the chief decion, "The Consul wants a cohort, he gets a cohort! Get me 500 men from the Tenth ready at 6:00PM assembled in full battle gear at the Water Gate." The decion saluted and left the room while the two centurions, Modilus and Nongilus began to dress for the assembly.

Soon, exactly 500 Roman soldiers in full battle dress were assembled in formation of ten decions of 50 men each outside the Water Gate. They were a formidable contingent dressed in leather breastplates lacquered in gold. Their shields were also lacquered wooden and circular. The exterior circle was gold, the interior circle was silver, but over the interior circle was the seal of Rome—hammered into leather circles. Each soldier wore a battle sword fully shined and gleaming. Each sword was placed in a sheath which hung over his back. At their sides, each soldier had a short sword in a sheath belted to his waist.

In front of the column, was a standard bearer carrying the golden eagle of Rome on a ten foot high shaft. To his side was another standard bearer carrying the pennant from the legion in which they served. He was accompanied on either side by two trumpeters with three foot long gleaming golden trumpets by their side. The men had formed into a column five abreast and were at attention.

In the front were twelve Temple policemen. They had been dispatched on the orders of the head priest Kaiaphas to accompany the cohort across the Kidron Valley to the Garden of Gethsamane to the site where Jesus and his band were to camp for the night. They were dressed in their uniforms and wore white tunics with a blue border belted at the waist. At their sides they carried a short spear. This was the largest weapon any Jew was allowed to carry under the Roman Occupation and was permitted only to the Temple police.

As the group began to assemble, an array of people from inside the city walls had begun to filter through the gate to see what was going on. It was the time of the Passover, and many of the pilgrims now crowded within the city walls. It was a cool pleasant spring night and mostly everyone was outside.

As the trumpets began to sound the marching chant and the drums began to beat out the cadence for the march. The soldiers lifted their shields and began to fall in step with the front rank. As they marched, they grunted as each left foot hit the ground and the decion called out the cadence to the beat of the drum. As the columns began to wind around the wall of the city toward the Water Gate, the Temple police fell in behind in a loose marching formation and roughly following the cadence and matching the strides of the Roman soldiers.

Alongside of either column, about two hundred of the people who had come out to watch the military array now followed the column and ran alongside. Some of the children were imitating the military bearing and attempting to match the grunts and stride of the Roman soldiers as they went. Some ran up ahead of the group. Many straggled behind.

As the cohort had assembled, the Centurion rode up on his horse and began to address them. "This day we have been given orders to cross the Kidron Valley in quick time cadence and to ascend the road to Gethsamane. At all times until further order, you are to march in formation and when directed to halt, you are to remain at attention. Until further order from me. You are not to engage in any confrontations with any civilians, unless ordered to do so. You are to ignore the words or actions of any civilians unless otherwise ordered by me." The soldiers sensed that something important was about to happen. They had just six days earlier marched in from Caeseria to fortify the Antonia Palace and were well aware of the possibility of action by an unruly crowd. On command, they could form a turtle formation with the exterior shields facing out and the interior shields forming a roof over the soldiers. Their spears would jut out of the slits between the shields. For now, they were more intent on intimidation. Fifty units of ten men could easily engage several thousand if they followed the much heralded Roman military discipline.

The crowd of many people marched down the slope to the Garden of Gethsemane. The Temple guard had moved to the front. On all sides, a motley crew of Jerusalem denizens kept pace. They were curiosity seekers, ragamuffins, beggars, and drifters of all sorts. It was Passover eve and the pilgrims and respectable residents of Jerusalem were at rest savoring their Passover meal and enjoying their families. They had just finished their Passover dinners, and had been outside as they saw the Temple Guard and a cohort of Roman soldiers forming into columns outside the Antonia Palace. The pomp and noise drew them forward. It was just growing dark.

Behind the Temple Guard contingent of twelve men came a cohort of 500 Roman soldiers all dressed in full battle array. At the corners of each decion, each man held torches aloft. The fires from the torches glinted on the gold on their shields and breastplates. In between each decion, a drummer banged out the march cadence. In between each drum beat, the soldiers banged their spears on their shields in counterpoint and grunted on the drumbeat. After every ten decions, a Centurion marched alongside the drummer. Within the second decion, Judas Iscariot was surrounded by soldiers as he trudged along to the beat, across the Kidron valley and up the hill to the Garden of Gethsemane.

The children following the procession imitated the soldiers march and pretended to carry swords and shields as the Romans. The rest of the crowd simply followed alongside to see what the spectacle was all about.

Slowly the march stretched across the Kidron Valley. After about 45 minutes, the lead Temple Guard reached the edges of the Garden where Jesus and his followers had spread out their cloaks and gear for the night. As the procession crept across the Kidron valley, many of Jesus' entourage began to fold up their belongings and slink up to higher ground. Only Mary, Peter, Andrew and a few of the others remained. As the Temple Guard approached, a clerk from the Temple stepped forward. Peter had been on alert for danger and drew his sword from under his cloak and swung in one motion. The sword bounced off the supervisory clerk's head and sliced his ear. Copious amounts of blood flowed down his side as he staggered back to the Temple Guard.

Behind the Temple Guard, the Roman soldiers spread out into 20 columns each behind the Temple Guard and filled in behind as they marched up the slope to the Garden. Soon, the entire cohort had assembled into a neat formation, with torches ablaze at the corners. Behind the second row stood Judas Iscariot. At the command of the lead Centurion, the center of the line separated and Judas was pushed to the front and stumbled to the ground. As he rose to his feet, he came to Jesus.

"I'm sorry, Master. It is as I said." He hugged and kissed Jesus; he knew it was the last he would see of him.

Jesus said. "I know. I understand."

With that, the leader of the Temple Guard was urged forward by the Centurions, "Are you Jesus the preacher from Galilee?"

"Yes, that is I." Jesus replied. "What do you want of me?"

"Come with us."

"Where are we going?"

"To the high priest's house."

"Am I under arrest? What is the charge?"

"We shall see. Please. This way."

Jesus looked around and saw that the rest of his followers would not be taken as well and began to walk with the Guard.

Judas was immediately surrounded by two decions of the Roman guard and marched off as well.

The military contingent began to snake along the route back across the Kidron Valley. It was now nearly midnight and the torches lit the way. This time there were no drums no marching sounds only the shuffle of marching feet in the dusty trail back to the city, each left foot in unison hit the ground followed by a grunt.

As they entered the city gate, the main forces went to the left to the upper city and the high priest's home. The twenty soldiers attending Judas marched him straight to the rear of Antonia Palace. Judas would not be seen alive in public again.

CHAPTER ELEVEN

Judas Questioned After Arrest of Jesus

JESUS' FOLLOWERS JUST STOOD dumbstruck at what had just happened. Had their hopes of Jesus' becoming the messiah and leading them out of the crushing burden of Roman rule been dashed? Or would he somehow have God come to his aid at the last minute? It began to dawn on them that, if Jesus had been arrested, then they all might be. Slowly they began to fade into the darkness of the olive groves in Gethsemane. Peter and Andrew followed close behind the trail of sightseers following the Roman column and did their best to blend in.

Judas was not so lucky. Several soldiers had peeled off from the column and grabbed Judas by the arms and rushed him off along a different path to the left and down the hill. In the commotion of the march of the cohort, and the shuffling of the crowd following, Judas' arrest and departure went unnoticed.

After being pushed and prodded along the path, the soldiers came to the rear of Antonia Palace. They threw Judas into the small enclosure and shut the door. Eventually, a Roman with two attendants came into the enclosure. Judas was bound to a chain as the Roman found him.

"You are Judas, the son of Simeon, who lives in the upper city."

There was no point denying it. "Yes."

"You are known as the Iscariot."

This was not a good start. The interrogator spoke clear Aramaic and had asked the question calmly enough. But it was the beginning of a bad night. "I don't know what you mean."

"Come now. We have followed you since you were involved in last year's uprising. You, and Bar Abbas, Thaddeus, Simon, and the others. We have followed you for the past year."

"But who…"

"Do you think we do not know? You are one of the sicarii and you have been a zealot."

"No…I…"

"Don't bother. We know. But what of this Jesus? You have many contacts with him, do you not?"

"Yes. I support his ministry. He is a very pious man. We have been friends for many years."

He had, in fact, been the treasurer for the Jesus group and had raised money often in Jerusalem for his missions among the faithful there. He would regularly bring provisions to the group on their travels. His activity in this regard was well known.

"Is he supported by the zealots? Are you his contact with the zealots?"

Judas was taken completely by surprise. He had not expected such a connection. "No…No…What? Jesus is not a zealot. He has no interest in rebellion. He is just a preacher."

"But you…you are a revolutionary. You and your band of bandits forment trouble against the Romans."

"No…No…I am a scribe."

"Yes…Yes…We know. We have followed you for a long time. And you have lead us to Jesus."

This was terrible. Jesus…his friend for many years…he had tainted with his own acts. What to say? What to do? "No…No…Jesus is just a Galilean preacher, he knows nothing of war, or Jerusalem politics. He is just an old friend whom I support in his ministry."

"All right then. What does he preach?"

"Generally…love. He tries to avoid violence, and asks Jews to repent and love thy neighbors."

"Have you trained him in rebellion?"

"Never. He has spent his life in study and preaching. He knows nothing of war."

"But he is called the 'King of the Jews,' he claims descent from David and he enters Jerusalem on a donkey with his followers laying palm leaves in his path."

This was getting worse. They had been following Jesus as well. "Look. He has no political or military aspirations. King David lived over a thousand years ago and had eight wives and many concubines. He probably had many children. Over a thousand years they intermarried many times. Probably every Jew could have some claim of descent from David. As for as his entry into Jerusalem…"

"You were there."

"Yes, of course. I support his ministry."

"You saw the donkey, and heard the hosannas."

"Yes. He was simply recreating an old story to draw attention to his entrance."

"Yes…Yes…We know. Fulfilling the prophecy of Jeremiah for a messiah. So he claims to be a messiah!"

"No. It was Zechariah, but messiah does not mean what you think. It just means one anointed to carry a message of salvation for the Jewish people. It does not mean a king or a military leader. Our messiahs are not kings. They were revered holy men who bring holy messages."

"And what is his message? Why did he disrupt the Temple court and overturn the tables of the moneychangers? Do you think we did not see that? The guards from Antonia Palace look down on the Temple Court every day."

"He wants to reform the religion. He seeks the truth…the true form of religion."

"What is this nonsense?"

"As you know, pilgrims come to Jerusalem to celebrate Passover. But they want to sacrifice animals in the Temple. As it has come down, they must be "pure" animals. Since the pilgrims come several days trek from their villages, they cannot bring "pure" animals, but must buy them here. The Sadducees certify the animals as pure and the Temple allows certain people to sell them. The coins used to purchase the animals must be Jewish coins without the heads of foreign rulers on them. These foreign coins are unholy because they carry images of men who wish to be worshipped as gods. These coins cannot be used for commerce in the Temple and must be exchanged for our Jewish coins at a great fee collected by the moneychangers. The Sadducees also license the moneychangers and grant them a space in the Temple courtyard. It makes Jesus sick to see all this fraudulent commerce taking place in the holy place, gouging the honest pilgrims, so he launched an attack on the entire practice to bring attention to what he feels is an abomination. It was a peaceful demonstration. Nothing more."

"But, this is dangerous rabble-rousing."

"No. Only a holy message."

"It would certainly benefit you and your zealot friends to take advantage of the commotion. You certainly support it. Now, does Jesus claim to be the Son of God."

"That is an old chestnut the Pharisees bring up. All of us are Sons of Men, all of us are Sons of God since he made us in his image."

"You have a clever reply for everything. We shall report this, and see what happens."

Judas slumped to the side of the hut. He knew he was a dead man, but he would never take Jesus down with him.

CHAPTER TWELVE

Jesus at Sanhedrin

GROUPS OF MEN WERE talking excitedly to each other at Kaiaphas' house. Many were old friends and greeted each other jovially at first and then began to talk in earnest about the business at hand. Generally, the Sadducees hung together. They were dressed in fine robes, high embroidered hats and were well groomed. They were the wealthy educated aristocracy that had for the past five hundred years had the exclusive hereditary right to manage the Temple and all its religious functions; but now they served the pleasures of the Roman Procurator who held the power to appoint the head priest or depose him. As a result, the appointed chief priest was viewed by many to be at the beck and call of the Romans. In some ways, however, the Sadducees tried to fulfill their role as the supreme religious leaders of the Jewish people and could often intercede with the Procurator where serious transgressions of Jewish law or affronts to Jewish sensibilities had caused a major unrest. The Sadducees sought to tread a fine line between the Jews and the Roman Procurator and to keep the peace. Among the Sadducees there were many factions, each of which sought power and supremacy within the Temple hierarchy. Some secretly consorted with the Romans and were their spies and toadies, others had strong religious convictions and sought freedom from the Roman abominations which controlled their country. The Sadducees to a man, however, would always insist on the principles which supported their hereditary rule. This all came from a strict and precise reading of the Torah—the book on which the Jewish nation depended. They controlled the Temple and the many employees and officers of the Temple. They insisted on regular pilgrimages by all Jews to Jerusalem for Temple worship on an annual basis. They insisted on animal sacrifices and complete obedience to the formal ritual requirements as well as payment of the tax to support the Temple. The control of the Temple naturally led to the admission to the Temple courtyard of the moneychangers and animal purveyors necessary for the ritual sacrifices. Only animals—doves, lambs, calves usually—who were deemed pure by the Sadducees as defined by the Torah. The Sadducees believed they did well by doing good.

The Pharisees had always viewed the Sadducees with distrust. In the late 500's BCE, after having defeated the Hebrews Nebuchadnezzar, ruler of the Babylonia, had forced the migration of the intelligensia and upper social levels of the kingdom of Judea, to live in Babylon. In this way, he believed there would be no further uprising from the Jews since the source of their leadership had been transplanted to a place where they could be closely watched. For about fifty years, they remained in Babylon, where they nonetheless prospered and maintained a strong relationship to their faith and their laws and practices. Soon, the Persians conquered the Babylonians and the Jewish exiles returned slowly over the following years to rebuild their country. The faith and rituals they had preserved over the years in captivity had grown stronger and more exacting than those who remained in Judea. The term for the returnees was "Perushim" which became Pharisees. The many pharisaic priests, not granted admission to the aristocratic ranks of the Sadducees, scattered throughout Judea and Galilee setting up their own synagogues and schools to administer to the Jews across the land. These men were dedicated, serious professionals who insisted on strict observance of Jewish laws as a means of gaining salvation. Jesus in the town of Nazareth had received the same education by the Pharisees as most Jewish boys outside of Jerusalem and was well versed in all they taught.

Obviously, there was great political enmity between the Sadducees and the Pharisees. Their continuous feuding, together with the excesses of the Jewish Hasmonean kings at the time, permitted the Romans simply to march into Judea and seize control of the entire country without a single battle or armed resistance of any kind. When the Roman occupation became intolerable, they blamed each other for their plights; but neither group could unite the people or advocate a rebellion against these hated Romans.

The scribes, a third faction at the Sanhedrin, were the laymen of some distinction elected to the Sanhedrin. Scribe was a broad term for the educated elite who performed many important functions; they drew up important letters, contracts, deeds, wills, marriage contracts, officiated at sales of large transactions, performed accounting functions and could mediate disputes. They were learned in the many Jewish laws and the commentary on those laws. Because they held no particular religious function, they often determined conflicts between the Pharisees and the Sadducees.

Despite their political differences and the disparities in their backgrounds and finances, the men greeted each other warmly since they had been through many meetings and resolved many disputes and criminal matters among themselves by diligent negotiation and well reasoned persuasion. Many respected their occasional adversaries, and accorded them respect in their discussions.

Eventually, Kaiaphas and his retinue entered the hall and the men sought out their assigned seats. Kaiaphas sat in the center of the front now surrounded by his father-in-law, the former high priest Annas and the other high level Sadducees.

Before he could get through a long preamble calling the meeting to order, Gamliel, a Pharisee, interrupted him:

"What are we assembled for, it is not a proper procedure on the eve of Passover to conduct any business. Besides, the full Sanhedrin has not been notified or permitted to attend. We will never reach a quorum..."

Kaiaphas interrupted him in turn. Gamliel was well known as a brilliant legal scholar who could launch into long interpretive analyses of the law. To let him get underway would only disrupt the meeting and allow no work to be completed.

"I know. I know. This cannot be an official assembly. It is not a hearing and we can take no action. This is an investigation. There

will not be a full Sanhedrin. This is the evening of ˼
no work can be attempted! We are aware of that. T˺
meeting called because we are facing a matter of e˸
which will require us to reach a consensus as to l..
seek your advice and wisdom, not your adversarial skills.

A buzz rose among the benches of the men assembled in the room. The whole procedure was highly irregular. It was Passover eve, now night, and the men wanted to return home to their families. Because of the many disparate groups on the Sanhedrin it was absolutely essential that every procedural rule, every long standing custom or ritual be observed. The Jews for over a thousand years had developed a complete body of law which governed nearly every aspect of their lives. Their adherence to these laws had preserved their community through centuries of hardships. But exacting adherence to the law had risen to a religious mandate which could not be altered or ignored. Besides, when one group suggested even the slightest deviation from the well-known rules, all other groups would view with great suspicion any actions which might come from the rule change. This convened assemblage was highly irregular. A meeting of the Sanhedrin was a serious violation because it took place not only at night but on the eve of Passover. The lack of a quorum, lack of notice and lack of any clear agenda were insurmountable obstacles to any action by the Sanhedrin.

Voices began to break out from all sides; each shouting their particular protest of the deficiency in the proceeding. Annas, now rose to stand next to Kaiaphas and held up his hands,

"Gentlemen, gentlemen. Hear us out! Please. We come in peace for your guidance. Hear us out!"

After several minutes, the assembly began to calm down. Kaiaphas started again:

"I will get to the point. Jesus has been arrested by the Romans and is now entrusted to our custody. We must decide what to do or the Romans may surely execute him. That is the problem. It is one that affects us all and we must decide how to present this to the Romans. Perhaps as a united body."

s the words left his mouth, stirrings, then mutterings and finally outs began to erupt from the assemblage.

"What? Arrested? When? How!!"

"What have you done now? It is your fault. You had him arrested."

"We can't let them do that!"

"He was a troublemaker, but arrest? How so?"

It took several minutes to calm everyone down and get silence once again. Kaiaphas stood making placating gestures.

"Gentlemen, gentlemen, friends. Let me tell you the story. Pilate demanded my presence for an important meeting. I came over to the Palace and he told me his spies (…he didn't actually say spies…) but they told him about Jesus' entrance on a donkey through the Water Gate surrounded by his followers, who threw palm fronds in his path and were singing 'hosanna!' You all know what that means! The messiah! What gall!

"Well, the Romans and their spies began following him. Of course he was preaching outside the Temple, but then Jesus led a raid on the Temple courtyard overturning the moneychangers' tables and shouting about reform, that it was a den of thieves.

"The Romans now claim he is calling himself the 'King of the Jews' and the Son of God. Now, they fear insurrection and want to make an example of him.

"I asked Pilate not to do anything hasty and to let me consult with you today to see what should be done. He agreed that the Temple guards must accompany the cohort out to arrest him. He also permitted us to have custody of him until this could be worked out.

"Apparently, they knew of his whereabouts and had already assembled a full cohort as we were speaking. They were in full battle dress and had their standards in place."

Again, there was a rising level of muttering and then clamor broke out. This time, Zahor, one of the Pharisees stood and his followers began to call for silence for him to speak.

"Kaiaphas, that is a fine story, but how do we know the whole thing wasn't your idea to begin with? We know the moneychangers provide you a nice income and an attack on them was an attack on you."

Kaiaphas was prepared for this question. "Yes of course we were angry but the loss was small to the moneylenders and they had already paid for their booths in advance in the Temple court. Yes, it is an affront to our position as priests of the Temple. But, death—no, we certainly wouldn't want to kill one of our own during Passover. And what could we charge him with? Trespass, troublemaking. Do you believe the Sanhedrin would even consider such a case? No. We would take this to a lower level court and make him pay for the damages. We don't want to punish a popular preacher. The Romans want him put to death as the leader of an insurrection. We sent the guards along to make sure he and his followers were not killed on the spot. You know he has zealots with him who are his bodyguards. There could have been bloodshed...On the eve of Passover...a popular preacher from Galilee...No. We couldn't risk having a riot put down with the Roman guards slaughtering unarmed pilgrims...On Passover...Never."

"But his followers do threaten you."

"Certainly. But so do you. You threaten us every day. We Jews always argue. We do it for a living and write it in the Talmud. We have always had prophets railing against us. This one is no greater than Jeremiah, or Micah. Dissent we know about.

"But now, we must get down to the matter at hand. Jesus is waiting in the next room. We have to return him to Pilate by morning. We don't have much time. Bring him!"

Jesus came in surrounded by six Temple guards. He was not bound. He was shown to a bench in the middle of the room and faced most of the assembled Sanhedrin.

Kaiaphas rose and spoke. "Jesus of Nazareth. You have been brought before us on an informal basis to answer our questions. I can assure you that this is a very serious matter involving both Jewish law and Roman law. Your answers and your cooperation may well decide your fate. Do you intend to cooperate?"

With this, several scribes arose. The other gave way to Michal the most learned of the scribes. "This is not proper procedure. He must have appropriate witnesses appear and he must be told of the charges against him. You cannot elicit a confession. You are ignoring the law.

You can't do this. That is not the law! A man cannot be convicted on his own confession."

"I know. I know. But the Romans believe he will cause a riot and a rebellion. He is as good as dead!"

"But the law is the most important. Our whole religion is the law. We are the people of the book." A general din arose as arguing factions broke down into separate confrontations.

Jesus spoke, softly to himself at first, then aloud. He stood and surveyed the assemblage. He was used to crowds and learned in the law. He knew they could do nothing to him because he had done nothing the Sanhedrin could fault him for. "What do you want to know?" A silence fell. He had their full attention.

"What is your name?"

"Jesus."

"Where are you from?"

"Nazareth."

"Who is your father?"

"Joseph."

"What did he do?"

"He was a tekton."

"From which tribe was he?" Jesus knew this was a trick question. He was a descendant of David, and thus had royal blood, but, after a thousand years, half of the Jews had David's blood in their veins. But the messiah, it was said, came from the regal line.

"He was from the tribe of Benjamin." He finished with a sigh. "He was a descendant of David." There was a stirring on the benches, but then they strained to hear again.

"What is your occupation?"

"I was trained as a tekton by my father and uncle, but for many years, I studied throughout the world. I am now a preacher." He was careful not to use the word rabbi. He was merely claiming to be in a longstanding tradition of itinerant preachers.

"I understand you were with John the Baptist at Bethbara. What did you learn from him?"

"He was a brilliant preacher who believed strongly in repentance and renewal, and used baptism as a ritual to signify the atonement."

"You do not baptize?"

"No. I do not, but I feel it was a very meaningful ritual for those that did."

"You were with the Essenes?"

"Yes. I learned much from them. They were very kind to let me live among them. They have a unique view of purity and wisdom."

"But you did not stay?"

"No, I did not feel the monastic life of self denial and isolation was what I wanted or was the right path for the Jewish people. I needed to reach the people with my doctrine. I have lived among Zoroastrians, Egyptians, Greeks and other peoples because I was seeking answers in my own way. I have only sought the truth."

"Do you claim to be the messiah?" The question dropped suddenly was unexpected and startled him at first. Although he answered that question many times, in this setting before these men, it was a shock.

"Those are your words, not mine." A claim to be the messiah was a serious statement. Many frauds had claimed to be, but the Sanhedrin had to be dealt with seriously. Only the formal saying of the secret name of God was actually blasphemy. No one claimed Jesus did that. The claim to be a messiah by itself was not a crime.

"But surely you seek to lead people and have them follow. Do you seek to save them from Roman occupation and re-establish the Kingdom of Israel?"

"I am not a military man. I have no army. Nor do I seek the kingdom of men, I seek to prepare men for the kingdom of God. I do not seek success on a material level."

Nicodemus, the scribe, tried to speak over the din. "Gentlemen, gentlemen!" Gradually, the conversations subsided and the men returned to their seats. "Gentlemen, we must decide what we are doing here. As you all well know, and as you ably quote when it is to your advantage, we are the people of the book, of the law. We try to govern ourselves by the law of the Torah, and the Talmud. We are not some ignorant tyrants governing by the political whim. We have procedures, precedents, we have ample guidance from the Talmud and years of commentary. This is clearly not a valid criminal procedure.

"Although we do not have any witnesses, the full Sanhedrin is not present, and we have not had any formal accusation lodged against this man, can we even approach the idea that he has committed the crime of blasphemy? No! He may be a messiah, but as he correctly notes, he cannot be a messiah until he has been anointed like Eli and Samuel and Nathan before. No one can anoint himself, he must be anointed. It is absurd to think that this man would be king, he is a preacher, not a general."

Over the course of the next few hours, various men raised issues they had heard from all sorts of people. His failure to observe the Sabbath, his healing by sorcery—all were dismissed as both hearsay or harmless. The raising of Lazarus from the dead was recounted at length, but Jesus' involvement was not actually established—only his presence.

One Pharisee recalled a remark that Jesus made about destroying the Temple and restoring it in three days. He was roundly mocked; he simple had not understood Jesus' use of a metaphor—that the Jewish religion was in men's hearts not founded on a Temple. What was in men's hearts could be recreated within three days, a building of stone could not.

In the end, after reviewing his conduct, this collection of some men from the Sanhedrin could find no crime had been committed under Jewish law. They were forced by their commitment to turn him over to Pilate.

CHAPTER THIRTEEN

Judas' Death

THE THREE DECIONS HAD walked from Potter's Field to the Antonia Palace and were admitted in the side door. They were directed to a side room where they waited for the court to be concluded. At the noon hour, Pilate and his entourage came through the door back to his apartments. One of his aides whispered to Pilate and he dismissed the rest of his entourage except General Gallicus.

Pilate sat next to the men with the general at his right shoulder. "Well, I hear it's done. This sicarii Judas is dead."

"Yes, your excellency, it is done. He lies now in the Potter's Field."

"How was this done?"

"He died from hanging and from a gash to his stomach."

"Both? Why both?" Pilate looked for answers to the General, who shrugged, and asked the men.

Without looking up at Pilate, one of the soldiers mumbled, "Well, he tried to break away and hide as we led him away outside the walls. So Hortinus was able to catch him and grab his arm. As he spun around, I stabbed him with my spear and he fell to the ground. We carried him to the tree and hung him by a rope, as you said. As General Asclipio instructed us, we placed the footstool below him and tipped it over to show he had hanged himself."

"Uh huh," Pilate grunted, looking at the General. "So he committed suicide by first stabbing himself with a spear and then hanging himself.

Or did he hang himself first and then stab himself with a spear. How did he do that?"

The soldier shrugged. "Your excellency...I..."

"Yes, you. This is not great. We must discredit this Judas. He is a member of the zealots and a sicarii. His group must be discredited. We own the Sadducees and have scared the Pharisees into silence. Now we must discredit Judas and put the blame for this preacher's death on him. That will divide his followers from Jesus. And what do you do? I gave specific instructions that Judas should commit suicide for betraying his friend. And what do you do? You put the whole thing back on us! Now get that body down. Now! And leave the noose around his neck. Put out the word that he betrayed Jesus to the high priest and took money for it. And put a blanket over the stomach wound. We can't have him commit two suicides."

"Yes, excellency."

"Oh! And even better, give that Kaiaphas the money to buy that Potter's Field and have him say Judas returned the money they gave him, but they could not keep the blood money so they dedicated the field for a burial ground for the poor. Better yet...Don't tell Kaiaphas about the involvement of Judas. Just have them make the field a cemetery for the poor and bury Judas in it."

"Yes, excellency."

"Now, don't foul me on this. I don't want a riot on my hands. Remember—he hung himself, you found his body and cut him down. Got that?"

"Yes, excellency."

"Remember, get our people busy. We want to get the word out. Judas betrayed Jesus, took money from the priests and gave it back because he felt guilty. The priests used the money to buy the pauper's burial ground. Got that?"

"Yes, excellency."

"Now get moving. No one knows where Jesus and Bar Abbas are hanging on the cross yet. So no riots yet. Let's keep this Judas' thing on the priests. We don't need trouble, do we?"

"Yes, excellency."

CHAPTER FOURTEEN

Pilate hears Sanhedrin reports and sends Jesus to Antipas

ARPALA, ONE OF THE high priests from the Temple, had waited outside the entrance to the Antonia Palace. The work day began at 6AM each day and the priest had been waiting for some time. Soon the doors were opened, and the priest admitted. He was shown directly to the courtroom. As he bowed to Pilate, who was already sitting on the throne, Pilate spoke first.

"Priest! I have already heard. Can't you people do the right thing for once?" Obviously, some of Pilate's spies sat in the Sanhedrin and had already reported its findings.

"But, your excellency...we cannot..." stammered the priest.

"Yes, yes, I hear. Send this Jesus to Antipas, it is his jurisdiction. Now go!"

Two soldiers ushered the priest out.

As the priest was leaving he could see Jesus being escorted brusquely to where Herod Antipas lived while Pilate took up residence in Jerusalem. The priest hurried to keep up with the procession as they entered Antipas' residence.

They all were escorted into the throne room where Antipas had already commenced his business day. Jesus was pushed to the ground in front of Antipas.

Antipas had been expecting this because a messenger from Pilate already stood in the throne room. Antipas had also some spies who sat on the Sanhedrin, but wished to hear this play out. "Priest, I see we have your prisoner. What has this man done?"

"Tetrarch Antipas. He is not our prisoner but a Roman one. He has been accused of… (with that the priest recited the litany of events running from the attack on the moneylenders to the claim of kingship, and everything in between.)"

Antipas had been raised in a political world and was shrewd in dealing with cases. His father Herod had been king of Judea, as a result of having great influence with the Romans, and, while he claimed to be a Jew, he was only a recent Idumean convert, and not liked or trusted by the Jews. After Herod's death, his kingdom was divided into four parts and his son was named "Tetrarch" over just one of the four which was principally the area of Galilee in the north. However, he preferred to stay in Jerusalem. He knew Pilate was setting a trap for him. Jesus was from Galilee and well liked there. For him to take serious action against Jesus would cause great difficulty, yet Jesus as a Galilean might be in his jurisdiction but his principal acts of criminality had occurred in Jerusalem—the south which was in Pilate's jurisdiction. Better that this problem—and any popular dissent fall on Pilate—not him. Better to duck the issue. But, first he would have his moment. Antipas fingered his breakfast of fruits and he sipped an early cup of wine, he sent the guards to fetch Jesus.

Jesus was brought in and seated on a low bench in the throne room.

"Are you a Nazarene?" He spoke in Greek to confound Jesus as a harmless peasant.

Jesus replied "Yes." In Greek.

"What are you doing in Jerusalem? Making trouble?"

"No. Your excellency, I am preaching the word of our God." Aha, the issue was joined. Would Antipas the Idumean rise to the bait and defend his status as a Jew? Did Jesus mean to include Antipas in "our" or was Jesus referring only to the rest of the Jews?

Antipas ignored the ploy. "I hear you entered into Jerusalem on a donkey with your followers chanting hosanna. This fulfills a prophecy of Zechariah of a king coming to save Zion."

So Antipas was prepared. He was not the indolent and indulgent son of Herod. He was at least an astute politician with a sense of self-preservation.

"Do you believe you are the king of the Jews? Do you seek to rule my kingdom?"

"No, your excellency, I seek to prepare men for the kingdom of God."

"What is this kingdom of God?"

"When justice and love will prevail. When all men shall seek peace."

"Ah, ok, very good. You do not seek to lead a rebellion against the Romans?"

"I am not a military man."

"Do you seek wealth and power?"

"No, I am a humble preacher who seeks to prepare men so that they may be saved."

Antipas had heard enough. While capable of arousing the people, he was not a threat. "I believe I have no jurisdiction here. Any accusations I have heard all occurred in Judea. My area to govern is the Galilee. Let Pilate try him."

CHAPTER FIFTEEN

After Antipas

AFTER THE DISMISSAL FROM Antipas' chambers, the decion formed his men around Jesus and marched the short distance back to Antonia Palace. It was now about seven o'clock in the morning. The soldiers stopped at the foyer and had Jesus sit while they waited. The decion entered the court and motioned to one of Pilate's retainers. When Pilate had finished the matter pending before him, the retainer came forward and whispered into Pilate's ear, motioning to the decion. The decion strode forward and saluted Pilate.

"Well," said Pilate. "What has Antipas done with this man?"

"He says that he has committed no crime in Galilee so he has no jurisdiction."

"What? He is a Galilean. Of course he has jurisdiction."

"Your excellency, I cannot say. Tetrarch Antipas bid us return him to you for judgment."

"Ah. He wishes to duck responsibility. I don't blame him after what an uproar he caused with John the Baptist. Alright, it's on me." Pilate pondered for a second. Then "alright, it's on me. Take him below and get a confession. Find out who his contacts are and why he is in Jerusalem." He flicked his hand motioning for the decion to leave.

The decion returned to his men and escorted Jesus into the dungeon below. It consisted of an open cavern below the Antonia Palace. The men threw Jesus onto a rock ledge and stepped back to permit the interrogator access to the prisoner. The interrogator was an old man dressed in a civilian toga. He calmly pulled a stool in front of Jesus.

"Who are you?"

"Jesus, son of Joseph."

"Where are you from?"

"A small town near Sepphoris."

"Why have you come to Jerusalem?"

"To preach to the pilgrims."

"What do you preach?"

"Repentance and love."

"Are you seeking to set off a rebellion?" Suddenly, a calm shot out of nowhere. Jesus was not rattled.

"No."

"Do you seek to expel the Romans from Judea?"

"No. I preach the law of Moses and the one true God. I wish to prepare men for the kingdom of God."

"Do you claim to be the king of the Jews?"

"No."

"Others say you are."

"I know. Those are their words."

An aide came up to the interrogator and handed him a scroll. The interrogator began to read the scroll and ask questions from it.

"Do you know Judas son of Simon?"

"Yes."

"Do you know him as Judas Iscariot?"

"I do not know him by that name."

"Does he give you money?"

"Yes. As many people do."

"Do you know 'Bar Abbas'?"

"I know no one by that name. To my knowledge, it is not an actual name."

"Is it a pseudonym for a zealot leader?"

"I do not know that."

The interrogation went on for an hour with the interrogator asking more questions to see which group Jesus was associated with. Jesus repeated that he had little or no relationship with any of the revolutionary groups such as the zealots or the sicarii. Unfortunately, Judas' name repeatedly arose and his contributions to Jesus' ministry were well documented. The Romans knew the dates of the trips and an inventory of the provisions. More telling was the fact that Jesus was Galilean and that area had been for years a hotbed of revolution.

Then the beatings and scourging began. For several hours, the soldiers alternated beatings and scourging with more questions. To no avail. Finally, the guards gave up after Jesus had passed out once again. The decion who had overseen the interrogation went up to Pilate and come up to him in his family quarters. As he entered the room, he saluted and waited for Pilate to recognize his presence.

"Well," Pilate testily barked. "What have we got?"

"Nothing, your excellency, absolutely nothing. He is very clever, but he won't budge."

"Alright. Bring him up to the Secretarium!"

"Yes, your excellency."

CHAPTER SIXTEEN

Jesus with Pilate

"EXCELLENCY, I MUST ASK if this is a criminal trial. I feel I have done nothing wrong. I have heard that Roman law is just, and considers both sides fairly. Am I now subject to this Roman law?" Jesus asked. He knew the rules and he wanted a public trial where he must be acquitted.

Pilate flinched in frustration. He knew Roman law had requirements. This man was entitled to a lawyer if he chose, and it was required that least two witnesses give personal eyewitness testimony against him. Yet, he was impatient. These Jews had tied up three legions to have their miserable little country of Judea. Only recently, Varus, his mentor, had lost three legions in Germania—utterly slaughtered by a clever ambush of the barbarian tribes. This annoying country produced precious little grain, and very little in taxes. Yet at every turn there was some group protesting, some terrorist activity and insisting on some religious term he did not understand. "Young man, you are very presumptuous. What makes you think you have rights? You are a terrorist. You would lead a rebellion. Now tell me, why do you meet with a known terrorist?"

"Who is that?"

"This sicarii. This Judas Iscariot."

Now we are getting somewhere. Pilate has gotten some information. It is useless to deny it but dangerous to admit it. "I have many followers, your excellency."

"Don't be obtuse. This man brings you money and food. We know this."

"Many have, your excellency."

"You wish to lead a rebellion."

"No, your grace. I am not a military man. I don't know how to fight or lead an army. I have no skills to govern and no use for temporal power."

"You wish to be king of the Jews."

"No, your excellency. I know nothing of governing. I have no need of power or material goods. I only seek to preach the law."

"You speak of the kingdom of God. You want your God to defeat our gods."

"My kingdom is not of this earth."

"What! What's this nonsense." Pilate fidgeted for a few seconds on the throne. "Take this man out and flog him. I want answers. Who are his contacts and what are his plans this holiday. Will there be an uprising?"

Two guards stepped forward and dragged Jesus from the room.

As he was lead away, Jesus thought. "Slow down. Think. Be calm and think." His heart was racing. Somehow he felt the rush of excitement, before he started to preach, the river of zeal coming up to his head. But with fear. He felt hot and cold at the same time. Here was a man who could kill him without a second's hesitation. He was clearly toying with him, like a hawk tormenting a squirrel. First he stabs with his beak, then he flips it over with his talons, as the squirrel struggles to regain its feet and run. Pilate was a hack politician who had risen through the ranks by gaining favor with his superiors while squashing those beneath him. He had no mercy, no pity. His only job now was to take as much wealth from Judea as he could and send enough to Rome to look good and keep as much for himself without being caught. He could never understand the Kingdom of Heaven, the one true god, mercy. His people ruled by superior military force, their sole objective was to extract taxes from conquered peoples. They could never absorb the culture of the conquered peoples—too weak to defend themselves—their wealth, their crops, their animals were all now property of Rome. Even their bodies; they could easily become slaves. Jesus thought "I cannot convert this man, I can't even speak to him. I must figure some way to escape. I cannot anger him—he only wants provocation to kill me. I cannot invoke pity—he will want to torture me for his own pleasure."

CHAPTER SEVENTEEN

Jesus—Second Visit to Pilate

ONCE AGAIN JESUS WAS thrown roughly to the floor in front of Pilate as he sat in court in the Praetorium. He was bloody from scourging and numerous blows to the face The centurion faced Pilate and saluted. Pilate had been eating from a dish of figs to his right. He threw a handful of figs at the centurion, who continued to stand at attention. There was a prolonged silence in the hall as Pilate glowered at Jesus.

Another prolonged silence. "Are you the king of the Jews? Are you the anointed one?"

"Those are your words." There was no good answer to these questions. Jesus knew no way out of this.

"My words, huh? Who do you think you are?"

"I am a preacher."

"Were you ordained?"

"No, sir."

"Are you a Sadducee or a Pharisee?"

"Neither, sir."

"Are you a zealot?"

"No, sir."

"How do you know Judas?"

"He is one of my followers, your excellency."

"But he is a sicarii!"

"I didn't know that."

"But he was in the revolt last year with Bar Abbas!"

"I wouldn't know that. I was in Galilee last year."

"But he gives you and your band food and money."

"I have many who do, your excellency."

This was going nowhere. "Alright, what do you preach?"

"I seek the truth."

"Gracious me! And what is truth?"

Pilate's tone was mocking. He was not open to a discussion of truth, nor could he comprehend Jesus' sermons or parables. There was no good answer. It would not do to throw pearls before swine.

"I'm sorry, your excellency. It would take some explanation."

"Yes, yes. I thought so. Look we are in a time of crisis. You Jews hold down three Roman legions in your miserable dust heap. We have rebellions every year. Your friend Judas was in one last year and we have followed him all the way to you. You are either a zealot or you would lead a rebellion. You are a risk. Take this man away and crucify him along with the others!"

"But, your excellency, this is not a trial, I have no lawyer and no witnesses against me."

"Young man, I am the voice of Rome and you create trouble. I don't need a trial."

Without more, Jesus was taken out to be crucified with the other prisoners.

CHAPTER EIGHTEEN

Arimathea Goes to Pilate

THE SUN WAS BEGINNING to break over the horizon of houses in the upper city of Jerusalem when Joseph of Arimathea and Nicodemus with the rest of the Sanhedrin came out of the front doors of Annas' house. It had been a grueling, wrenching meeting as the leaders of Israel had torn at Jesus with questions as to his ministry, his message, his intentions, his connections to the Zealots, and to all the other splinter sects. Jesus had held up well; he fielded the questions, often impertinent, often repetitive, with a calm good humor. Occasionally, when confronted with a particularly galling question, he would deliver a barb that would sting the poser into a red faced submission. As to his political ambitions, he had none. As to his military ambitions, he had none. He was able to deflect questions as to his messianic abilities, by simply saying, it was not his place to decide who the messiah was or would be but God's. As to what people thought, that was their opinion. He would return to his basic message, the tracts of his ministry were: love God and treat your neighbor with love.

Now, Jesus would be turned over to Pilate. What would he do?

Joseph and Nicodemus began to walk down the street to Nicodemus' house in the upper city. Mary Magdalene, Jesus' mother, and Lazarus had come in from Bethany when news of Jesus' arrest reached them from Joseph's servant. They had come to Nicodemus' house where they now awaited news of the Sanhedrin meeting.

As they came in the front door, Joseph and Nicodemus found the group from Bethany sprawled out on the couches and Lazarus covered by a heavy robe on the floor. They began to stir, rubbing their eyes and stretching. Mary Magdalene sleepily asked, "Well, what happened?"

Joseph answered. "Nothing so far. The whole Sanhedrin thing turned out to be a farce. There couldn't be trial. While the Sadducees were angry about the whole event in the Court the other day, it was not a serious crime. Then some of the others tried to see if Jesus was interested in creating a rebellion, but it was pretty obvious he was not."

"I could have told them that." Mary barked. "How could they think that?"

"They seem to think this talk about him being a messiah, means he's a wartime leader who wants to be king."

"Aie! They don't get his message."

"All this talk about the poor getting their rewards sounds like revolutionary talk."

"But, he means the kingdom of God. The revolt is in men's hearts."

"I get that, and you get that, but many in the Sanhedrin don't get that, and I'm afraid the Romans won't either."

"Why do they object even if he were the warlike messiah?"

"They don't want to stir things up and have the Romans kill more people. I'm afraid the Pharisees agreed with them."

"Ah. They like things the way they are?"

"Happens so."

"What happens now…?"

"He goes before Pilate."

"We should go to Pilate and tell him a thing or two!"

"Pilate's hearing will be behind closed doors."

"Let's go there anyway. Sitting here isn't doing any good."

"Alright, then, let's go."

With that, Nicodemus' wife came into the room with some breakfast. Some grabbed up the fruits and took a quick swig of milk and bolted out the door. As they paced up to the Antonia Palace, there were a few stragglers on the streets as the sun of early dawn began to break over the western city. The day of Passover was quiet and traffic was light.

Then over to the left, a rumbling was heard. A group of Roman soldiers were marching in the opposite direction. As they approached, it was clear that a prisoner was in the middle of ten Roman soldiers, marching quietly. The prisoner was…Yes, it was Jesus.

Joseph and the others hastened over towards the soldiers, and asked the decion what they were doing with the prisoner.

"Please stand aside and do not interfere." The decion looked grim and the soldiers had begun to draw their short swords.

"We mean no harm. Where are you going?"

"To Herod Antipas. Please disperse!"

Herod Antipas. But why him? Was Pilate avoiding this problem? He never gave anything to Antipas. The Romans considered him an irrelevant nuisance who ignored his responsibility governing the Galilean region. Why Antipas—that lout?

Joseph and the others followed behind the soldiers and mumbled questions among themselves. In the short distance to Antipas' temporary quarters, they could see the soldiers and Jesus swallowed up inside the mansion Antipas now occupied until he could reclaim his quarters in the Antonia Palace when Pilate and his entourage left.

Of course, the group was denied access to the mansion. They slumped around the roadway, and munched on the fruit they had taken from Nicodemus' house. Again, they began to debate what Jesus had done and what possible fate lay in store for him.

In less than half an hour, the Roman soldiers reappeared with Jesus, again in formal marching formation with Jesus in the middle.

Mary Magdalene shouted "Jesus, what happened?"

Jesus replied, "Nothing. Antipas refused jurisdiction. It seems they thought that because I was from Galilee that he should try me. He declined."

The decion now glowered over at the group as he marched by. "No more talk! You may be arrested!"

The group followed silently behind the soldiers the short distance back to the Antonia Palace. Again, the soldiers and Jesus were swallowed up behind the gates of the Palace. Again, they sprawled around the entrance. The sun was still low in the early morning sky. What would happen now...?

About then, Nicodemus' wife and two daughters came up the road to the Antonia Palace carrying baskets of food for breakfast. "I didn't want anyone to starve, God forbid. Please eat, enjoy!" Sitting on a sheet spread under a tree nearby, everyone sat and ate the food mostly in silence. There was nothing to say. Their beloved Jesus was now in front of Pontius Pilate, the Roman procurator who had power of life and death over him. What he had done, or may have done did not matter, it was what Pilate chose to believe—no more, no less. The streets were still only lightly traveled. It was a holiday and most people were home with their families.

Finally, the doors to the gate of the Palace opened and several guards took positions at attention. Joseph ran to the guards and asked to see Pilate. He gave his name while the rest of the entourage huddled behind him.

Soon thereafter, a scribe from Pilate's court came to the gate, "Joseph, follow me. His excellency will see you!"

Joseph turned to one of his men and took a small pouch and placed it in the pocket of his robe. He turned and followed the scribe into the antechamber just off the praetorium. Only he and Pilate were left to discuss matters in private. Joseph took the pouch from his pocket and slid it across the marble top to Pilate, who snatched it up with interest.

"Excellency, it is extract from the clams the Phoenicians tend. They produce the blue dye that is so highly prized for that rich royal color."

"Ah Joseph. Most kind. What can I do for you?"

"You have in custody a dear friend of one of my family members. This Jesus—the preacher from Galilee. Can anything be done for him? My sister's daughter is in love with him."

"Uh huh. Mary of Magdalene no doubt. We heard they were married. Yes he is in my custody. As you know, he was arrested last night and tried by the Sanhedrin. You are on the Sanhedrin, what happened there...?"

"Of course, when we heard that you and Kaiaphas were concerned about him, we took great pains to find out why. He is apparently a very popular preacher in Galilee who came to Jerusalem to gain more followers."

"But what of this incident at the Court of the Temple where he disrupted the whole sacrifice practice. What of that?"

"He, like many reformers, objects to many things associated with the Sadducees. The whole sacrifice ritual has been opposed by many for years as an unnecessary remnant from our pagan neighbors. But the Sadducees control the sacrifice and the Temple and do very well at the expense of the superstitious Jewish peasants. I think he was protesting the whole institution—the sacrifice, the Sadducees, and their control. He wants to have men have a more direct contact with God and not have to pay through the nose to some greedy priests."

"Uh huh. Is he a Zealot?"

"Jesus? No. Never. He is a man of peace. It would be against his nature."

"Does he claim to be the messiah?"

"I can't really say. Many people say so, but I have not heard him."

"Does he seek to be the king of the Jews?"

"No. I can't see that. I think he believes he is a prophet, especially for the poor and needy. We have a long tradition of such prophets."

"Well, Joseph. I'm afraid that we found he has a connection to a Zealot and a sicarii—a Judas. Judas was active in the revolt last year and we have been keeping an eye on him for some time now. He delivers money and provisions to this Jesus and consorts with his followers."

"That's true. I did not know he was a sicarii. He comes from a very nice family."

"We've investigated all that. Yes he dresses nicely and has his hair oiled and speaks with an educated Judean accent. But he stands out like a sore thumb when he goes to see these crude Galilean bumpkins that follow this Jesus.

"No, Joseph. I am afraid I cannot let Jesus off. He has come into Jerusalem in the midst of your Passover when the city is crammed with pilgrims. I have brough in two legions from Caesarea to keep the peace. But, your Jesus has gone too far. I could allow some streetside preaching, but he has gone too far. I don't trust his relationship with Judas and the Zealots, and I didn't like this disturbance in the Temple Court the other day. People call him the messiah and the king of the Jews. I can't take the chance. Rome would have my head. I have ordered him crucified."

Joseph was stunned. It had already been decided. He sat back and tried to regain his composure. What could he say? What could he do? What would the family say?

"Could you give me a few minutes, your excellency?"

"Of course, Joseph. I wish there was something I could do."

Ideas sprang into Joseph's head. What to do?

"Perhaps there is something, your excellency."

"Name it."

"I own a worthless plot of ground just outside the city called Golgotha. Could we give Jesus a private crucifixion on that ground? It would not attract crowds and would be easy for your soldiers to control."

After some thought, Pilate nodded. "Alright. I see no harm in that. Few security problems. No crowds. But I have two other bandits I am going to have crucified as well. We would need to do all three together."

"That's no problem for me.

"I also have a family tomb just off the Golgotha field. We could lay Jesus there after he dies. I don't think the family could bear up if he hung on the cross and rotted for days."

"That's fine. If he's dead, I can't see the harm." Pilate turned to his bell and rung for the scribe. "Crispio. Tell the soldiers to take the prisoners to Golgotha for crucifixion. When Jesus is dead, let Joseph here take his body for burial in the family tomb."

"Understood, your excellency."

"I'm sorry Joseph that your friends must suffer this matter, but I am afraid he brought it on himself."

"I understand, your excellency. Thank you for your understanding."
Joseph was shown out the front gate to where Mary and the others had gathered. He was devastated as he looked at all the upturned

faces, but they could already tell it was bad news. Joseph could not even attempt to hide how he felt.

"Mary, Lazarus…Pilate has ordered him crucified. There was nothing I could do."

Before he was finished, the women began to shriek. They staggered over to the shade of the tree and collapsed on the sheet.

Mary his mother could only mumble "Why him? He could have had a nice life…he chose this…"

Lazarus stood hands on hip and stared off into space, afraid to look at anyone.

Mary Magdalene collapsed and hid her face in Martha's breast and sobbed quietly.

The whole scene was devastating. The Romans, those brutal Romans, with the worst brutal punishment the world had ever seen to their gentle, smart boy. So bright, so idealistic, caught up in the harsh material world of politics and power. He had such hopes. But why this cruel disaster?

The group eventually began to collect itself and wander to the rear of the Palace to join Jesus en route to Golgotha. As they got there, Jesus emerged with the crosspiece of the cross tied to his shoulders along with two other prisoners. Ten soldiers and their decion surrounded the prisoners as they left the basement of the palace.

Jesus looked awful. He had been whipped and punched. His face was swollen and his nose was bloody. Streaks of bloody whip marks crisscrossed his back and chest. He wore his robe tied around his waist and stumbled forward under the weight of the crosspiece. After a few more steps, he fell to the cobblestones. Joseph motioned to Simon of Cyrene to come forward and help with the cross. He helped Jesus up and took part of the load on his shoulders. One of Mary's friends stepped forward to wipe his face. The procession weaved down the narrow streets until they left by the small rear gate outside the city. Golgotha was just another 100 meters. When they got there, the prisoners were ordered to lie on their backs on the ground, while the soldiers dug the holes for the upright pieces, the stipes. The ends of the stipes had already been whittled to a point to have the cross piece fitted into it while bearing the prisoner.

It was almost 9:00AM as Jesus and the others began to emerge. The prisoners each carried their patibulum across their backs. This would serve as the cross piece on which their arms would be tied and from which their bodies would dangle, slowly sucking air out of their lungs. He had had little sleep and little to eat. As he tried to bear his span of wood, he limped and occasionally stumbled.

Joseph immediately walked up to the centurion Escalonus—a familiar face who was usually stationed in Jerusalem.

"Good morning, Escalonus."

"Well, not so good for you, sir." Escalonus said with an apologetic smile.

"Nonetheless, it's good to see you in charge. This man is my niece's husband and she has been suffering greatly." He motioned to Mary Magdalene. "Perhaps, you could take some care with him."

"I understand, even Pilate has ordered special care, sir. He is to be crucified just up ahead and not on the highway. The men are digging the holes for the stipes (upright poles) as we speak."

At this point, Jesus stumbled and fell, looking up at Joseph. Joseph nodded recognition as did Lazarus. The guards stooped to help Jesus up and he joined the procession with the other two prisoners.

Other soldiers had lain three stipes on the ground in front of three holes. As the procession reached the stipes, Escalonus directed the prisoners to lay the patibula perpendicular to the stipes and to stand back. The soldiers had finished digging the holes and began to insert the stipes into notches in the three patibula. Once they were securely fixed, the prisoners were directed to lie supine on the stipes with their arms extended. The soldiers then tied their arms securely into the patibula. Some of the soldiers hoisted up the tau shaped cross, while others slid the bottom end into the holes. Others still pulled on ropes to pull the stipes into an upright position. As the stipe slid into the hole, the other soldiers began to hammer stakes around the stipe to wedge it into an upright position. Finally all three men dangled by their wrists on the upright crosses. On each stipe was a small board nailed perpendicular to the stipes on which the prisoners could rest their feet from time to time. However, it was just below the spot where they could push themselves up comfortably. They could barely reach it to give themselves temporary relief. With that, the soldiers formed a perimeter around the crosses with their lances upright. It was 9:00AM, the ram's horn sounded in the distance.

One of the guards offered Jesus and the other men a sponge of sour wine—like vinegar—mixed with water. Jesus had been told in advance not to accept this sponge because it would heighten his senses and make the pain more acute. As the guard backed away, the women were allowed inside the guards to attend him. The pole was about 9 feet high so Jesus' head was about 3 feet from the women. Mary his mother began to pray and the other women began to kneel. Eventually, Jesus tried to comfort them.

As the sun rose and past the noon height, Jesus' breath was becoming ragged as he struggled awkwardly to rest on the small foot board. By this time, no angry crowd had appeared and the guards grew more lax in their security. They were bored with three hours of this somber scene

Joseph and Nicodemus were permitted inside the perimeter of the guards, and eventually Lazarus and some Essenes were as well. Jesus looked up at Nicodemus—a Pharisiac mentor of his. "God forgive them for they know not what they do." Nicodemus knew from long conversations that they had that Jesus felt his death would do little now to bring justice and peace to the world. The Kingdom of God was an eventuality that man would reach at some future time and that empires like Rome were doomed. Nicodemus and Joseph knelt and prayed.

The soldiers led by Escalonus began to approach the three prisoners with a crucifragium—a device used to break the legs of the prisoners so they could no longer seek respite on the foot boards. Joseph who had been chatting for a while previously with Escalonus, again engaged him in a discussion.

"Escalonus, I realize that now is the time to break the leg bones, but I request that you not do this to Jesus. His family is in attendance and would be very upset to see this. I would be most grateful."

Escalonus looked up and halted the men. "<u>Most</u> grateful, sir?"

"Yes, most grateful." Yes, Joseph would be most grateful.

Normally, a prisoner would take several days to die on the cross, suffering in public a horrible agony. The soldiers assigned to guard duty were not anxious to spend all that time, in idle observation until the men actually were dead. The hastening of their death was a welcome remedy. What Joseph was asking was a very special dispensation. Escalonus was well aware that Joseph was a wealthy merchant, who had been favored by Pilate, to change the site of the crucifixion to Joseph's own land near his own family sepulcher.

"Very well, I think I can spare a few hours."

By 3:00PM, Jesus was tired and breathing heavily. He was able to croak out, "I thirst." Lazarus beckoned to Escalonus and asked if they could offer Jesus something to drink and indicating he could be most grateful.

With Escalonus' blessing, Lazarus offered Jesus a wet sponge saturated with sour wine and some gall. Jesus drank and nodded gratefully to Lazarus and then his head almost immediately sunk down onto his chest. He slowly lost consciousness and stopped breathing.

The guards came up to examine Jesus. They signaled to Escalonus that the prisoner was dead. Escalonus also checked Jesus' vital signs and agreed. It had been an extremely short crucifixion—six hours was unheard of, two days more likely.

Joseph, standing near Escalonus and hearing the pronouncement, said, "Pilate had promised us the body to place in the sepulcher before nightfall. Could we have the body?"

Escalonus dispatched a soldier to Pilate with the news and Joseph's request. When he returned with Pilate's authority, Joseph and Nicodemus began to take the body of Jesus from the cross. With the help of Lazarus and several of the women, the body was carried to Joseph's family sepulcher which was in a cave in the nearby hill about 50 yards away and laid Jesus to rest on some cloth.

It was the burial custom of the Jews that the body would lie still for several days at which time the female relatives would wash and dress the body with certain herbs to hasten the decay of the flesh and limit the odors. For the present the body would lie on the table in the sepulcher with the women to return later. After the women had fully prepared the body, it would lay at rest for about a year until the flesh had completely rotted from the bones. At that time, the bones would be placed in an ossuary which was then placed in a shelf of the sepulcher. For the time being, there was nothing to do but go back to Bethany and wait a few days. The procession trudged off at a mournful pace. Joseph remained behind to direct the men rolling the large stone over the mouth of the sepulcher. He, Lazarus and Nicodemus then held an earnest discussion for some time with three Essenes in their gleaming white robes, before all departed.

CHAPTER NINETEEN

Mary Magdalene at the Tomb

AFTER THE SABBATH WAS over, Mary Magdalence, Jesus' mother and Martha and several servants began the ride from Bethany to Golgotha at first light. The mood was somber and the conversations muted as the donkeys picked their way along the road. Their dreaded task was to wash and anoint the dead body of Jesus. As Jerusalem came into view, the women could feel again the pain of that day when Jesus hung by his arms just a few feet above them on the cross. They made the turn around wall of the city and could see the short distance to the crosses which still bore two of the revolutionaries and the empty stipe of Jesus' cross. Next they approached Joseph's family sepulcher and began to see an unbelievable sight. The massive stone had already been rolled aside from the entrance to the cave and several men of the Essenes were sitting on boulders near the entrance. Mary Magdalene jumped from her donkey and ran to the entrance. It was empty! The shelf on which Jesus had been lain just three days before was empty. The entire tomb was bare and quiet. Only his burial shroud lay on the shelf. As the Magdalene rushed back out to confront the men, the other women were coming up behind her.

"What have you done with him? Where is the body? What is happening?" Dozens more questions exploded from Mary as the other women began to understand what had happened. They went in to look for themselves and came out equally astonished. The Essenes stood quietly and tried to comfort them.

"We cannot help you now. It must be a time for quiet." Somehow, the men in the dazzling white robes of the Essene community had an almost priestlike solemnity. As Mary Magdalene and Martha began to absorb what they had seen, they sat on the ground and stared off into the distance.

After a time, Mary Magdalene rose and, in a distracted fashion, began to mutter. "Lazarus…Lazarus." The other women trailed behind looking quizzically at each other. "I must find Joseph. Where is Peter? What is going on?"

CHAPTER TWENTY

Isaac and Nicodemus

ISAAC TOOK THE SHORT walk from the lower city house which he shared with three other young men, up to the edge of the upper city to Nicodemus' house. While not wealthy, Nicodemus was a well-to-do scribe and respected scholar. He had served for many years on the Sanhedrin and was a close personal friend of many of those in power in Jerusalem. Among his close friends were Joseph of Arimathea, Kaiaphas the Chief Temple priest and many of the learned pharisaic Rabbis. He had met with Jesus prior to his crucifixion and discussed at length his ministry and theology. He joined with Joseph of Arimathea in supporting him. Unfortunately, he aided Joseph in actually removing Jesus from the cross and placing him in Joseph's family burial cave.

Isaac was a local melamed—a teacher of the boys prior to their Bar Mitzvah; but he had developed an irresistible urge to find out the details of this much celebrated Jesus and separate the fiction from the fact. He had tried to speak to James, Jesus' brother, and Peter as well as the other disciples but they were too suspicious of him or his motives to speak. Many of the disciples had left Jerusalem over the past few years and were not available in any case. Isaac was tall and thin, in his late twenties, and walked with the forward leaning stoop of a scholar. Normally he helped a spice dealer keep track of his stock, but today, he pursued his love, the lure of scholarship and history.

As Isaac came to Nicodemus' door, he was greeted by Nicodemus' wife. It was early afternoon and a cool spring day. "Ah, Isaac, he is expecting you. Come in."

The house was similar to most in the upper city, a sturdy two-story with an open air roof deck. It was surprisingly sparsely furnished but had racks of scrolls along the walls as if it were a library. Nicodemus came in and had Isaac follow him to the rear of the building, near the small garden. A long table ran the entire length of the rear wall up to the doorway. A brazier and several torches lit the room. A number of scrolls and papyri lay on the table. Nicodemus motioned Isaac to one chair and he took another. Nicodemus was elderly now and squinted at Isaac through heavy eyebrows. He had an immense gray beard which now covered his entire face. A cap sat atop his balding head.

"You know, young man, what you are doing is dangerous."

"Yes, Master. I understand. But if one doesn't try, one never succeeds."

"Well said. First, I have a letter from the latest Bar Abbas vouching for your credentials. The latest Bar Abbas was crucified with Jesus, but the zealots are still active and keep track of spies and turncoats. Whoever was able to contact them on your behalf and get them to give me this message must have their trust. They urge me to trust you as well."

It was now ten years since the crucifixion. Pilate was recalled to Rome and was replaced by the Roman governor Festus—widely viewed as harsh and incompetent. James, Jesus' brother, was the suspected leader of the followers of Jesus in Jerusalem. He was well-respected for his scholarship and piety and kept in touch with the disciples who had scattered from Jerusalem after the crucifixion. A Paul or Saul had apparently started to preach in the synagogues and villages of Asia Minor about Jesus. There were rumors of angry disputes between James and Paul.

A number of stories and rumors had begun to circulate about Jesus following the crucifixion. Huge angry debates could be heard almost daily. This had attracted Isaac and impelled him to seek out the true history. He would be the first to write the official story. Everywhere he turned, he was rejected. There was a heavy blanket of secrecy covering the story, and the disciples. Now, Isaac sought out Nicodemus—a man known for his veracity and scholarship.

"Now, how did Jesus die so soon on the cross? I am told it was just six hours."

"Now, certain areas are off limits. I cannot and will not discuss the events of the crucifixion. That is too dangerous an area for any sane man in Jerusalem. The best I will say is that Jesus was crucified by the Romans, Joseph and I took down his body from the cross and placed it in Joseph's family sepulcher. Since then, his body has disappeared. Those are the public facts and I support them. Yes. They are true."

"I notice you said 'his body' and not 'his corpse,' did you mean anything by that?"

"Did I? I'm sorry my translation back and forth from Aramaic to Greek and back is slipping."

"But 'body' means he was not necessarily dead."

"I can't speak to that."

"Some of the disciples claim to have seen Jesus in Ephesus, and other places. Could he be alive?"

"I can't speak to that. Hmm. Ephesus, you say. Interesting!"

"Other people have seen Mary Magdalene in Egypt."

"Possible. After the crucifixion, many of his followers left for cities in other countries. You know, about 40% of Jews live outside Judea and Galilee."

"Some say Mary went across North Africa to Spain."

"Could be. Many Jews are settled there."

"Was she Jesus' wife?"

"I really can't speak to that."

"Why all the secrecy?"

"I don't have to tell you that the Romans are on the lookout for any information about Jesus and his followers. Pilate was very anxious in those days, and his successors still fear a revolt. Pilate's mentor, Sejanus, was just killed off by Tiberius, and was recalled and never heard from again. I think he was chastised for the Samaritan slaughter. The Samaritans planned a big convocation on Mount Gezirim—just a religious event—but Pilate had his troops kill 10,000 people it is said. Many of them were actually crucified."

"But what about Jesus' body. It seems to have vanished. Does anyone know about that?"

"I can't speak to that."

"But you put it in the tomb."

"True. And I saw the soldiers roll the rock over the entrance."

"But you saw it empty, too."

"True again. Mary was standing at the tomb with several Essenes and Peter. And the tomb was empty. I saw that much."

"Where did he go? Who would want his body?"

"Good question. The body has little value in Jewish thought. After death, the soul leaves it, and the body is an empty shell."

"Paul and the others claim that body rose physically up to heaven. He claims God reclaimed Jesus to sit beside him in heaven."

"That's preposterous. We do not believe in physical resurrection anywhere in Judaism. The Pharisees believe the souls awake in the Kingdom of God, but only the souls. No Jew would ever make a claim for the physical resurrection especially soon after death."

"Some claim Jesus was the Son of God and is to be worshipped as a God."

"I have heard those claims."

"You spoke with Jesus, what did he say?"

"He only told me he was a simple preacher who sought to prepare men for the Kingdom of God. He asked that they be reborn—in much the same way John the Baptist did—by starting a new life of piety, repentance and good works."

"Well then, let me ask you about the events after the crucifixion."

"There are spies and informants everywhere. It also spelled the end for Pilate when the Samaritans complained to the Syrian governor and Rome. Pilate was recalled from his post. A little too late to save Jesus, however.

The disciples continued to meet somewhat secretively in Jerusalem, but mostly scattered to the rest of Asia Minor, to continue to preach the message of Jesus."

"What was the message of Jesus?"

"To tell the truth, I am not quite sure in a philosophical sense. It was mainly directed at the poor, to give them hope. In some places, I believe his words were interpreted to mean that he was the messiah and that the Kingdom of God would appear very soon. As a result, everyone had very little time to repent, atone and prepare for Judgment Day. At other times, I believe he sought to downplay all that speculation. He may have thought like Jeremiah, that our present problems were caused by our own bad acts and a breach of our covenant with God. Good behavior and greater piety would help rescue us from our plight. In our discussions, he felt we should seek to be 'born again.' By that I think he meant something like John the Baptist—renew, repent, atone and we would be renewed. He used a number of terms which I had difficulty understanding."

"Was he interested in a revolt?"

"No."

"Did he want to be king?"

"No. Not at all."

"Why did Rome kill him then?"

"I think it was a big misunderstanding and an overreaction. Jesus' past was totally unknown. He was associated for the first time with John the Baptist, but developed a big following very quickly in Galilee.

"He apparently had some help from the zealots and, in particular, Judas."

"Were the Pharisees against him?

"No. He was raised by the Pharisee priests. He followed them for the most part, but also felt they were excessive in their strict attention to the letter of the law; but that was all part of our tradition of debate. He was doing what we all do; we debate the meaning of things, of Torah, of law. You know how we are."

"So what was he?"

"He was his own man. He was unique. No one controlled him."

"But why crucify him?"

"It's hard to say. I mean he was crucified with Bar Abbas and another zealot. They might have thought he was associated with the zealots.

"In Rome, Sejanus was a favorite of Tiberius and Pilate was a favorite of Sejanus. Sejanus was known for his anti-Jewish attitudes.

"I always thought Jesus would get a trial after the Sanhedrin released him to Pilate. I think Pilate got his bluff called when the Sanhedrin and then Antipas refused to take action and he could not afford a public trial. That would have brought the Jews together. I really don't know."

"But what of his followers who believed that he was the messiah and Judgment Day was coming?"

"Some of them now believe he was the Son of God and that he was sacrificed for our benefit. We don't have a tradition of human sacrifice. That's clear from the story of Abraham, but the pagans do have this dying young god tradition. It is gaining great popularity among the converts. The Jews however will never accept it."

"How do you reconcile this with God? I mean you are a Jewish scholar and participate in the Mishnah. What do we think this was? Did God intend this, or is this just one of his mysteries?"

"Some say it was simply a colossal error. A huge calamity. Perhaps, the Jews are destined to suffer from these calamities from time to time. Others see the Jews as the chosen people as the messengers of the Kingdom of God who must suffer from time to time as God's servants. It is difficult to say. We seem to survive, but we suffer. Who knows what God has in store for us."

Isaac sat for a few more minutes, composing his notes. He began to shake his head. "Well, thank you, Master. I certainly appreciate your time. I wish I had more answers."

"Young man, perhaps some things are left buried. Or should I say, unburied."

Afterward

WHILE THIS BOOK IS a novel—a fictitious account of the life of Jesus, I have tried throughout to remain as faithful to current academic scholarship on the subject of historical Jesus. For inspiration, fact-checking, and insight, I am indebted to a number of books and authors I have identified below:

The Trial and Death of Jesus, by Haim Cohen, a Justice of the Supreme Court of Israel

Constantine's Sword, by James Carroll

Many books by Bart Ehrman

Many books by Géza Vermes

The Jewish War, by Josephus

Bloodline of the Holy Grail, by Laurence Gardner

The Gospel of Mary

The Gospel of Judas

The Dead Sea Scriptures, by Theodor H. Gaster

Jesus and Yahweh, by Harold Bloom

The Passover Plot, by Dr. Hugh J. Schofield

Richard D. Malmed

CPSIA information can be obtained at www.ICGtesting.com
Printed in the USA
BVOW11s1603271015

424182BV00001B/1/P